'Very cautiously, Gussie started the long climb down. He had a strange, empty feeling; he knew what he had just seen had happened, but he could not quite believe it.

The head came up again. This time it bobbed well out of the water, the shoulders, too. The man must be a very strong swimmer. He held his breath as the head and upper torso bobbed towards the same tilted slab it had been washed off two minutes before. Another wave came, tumbling white. The man went with it. When the wave receded, he was still there, crawling like a fly.

Gussie cheered. Then his heart seemed to roll over in his chest, and his skin prickled horribly.

*One of the man's legs was gone.*'

Gussie Smith should never have got involved on that fateful day – and he certainly shouldn't have fished Arthur Hopcraft's tin leg from the sea and returned it to its rightful owner. For Gussie is already in deep trouble with slimy Snell, the Truant Officer, and now 'Pegleg' plumps him into a series of extraordinary and highly alarming disasters . . .

# PEGLEG
## Sam Llewellyn

Illustrated by Robert Bartelt

**CORGI BOOKS**

# PEGLEG

## A CORGI BOOK  0 552 524891

Originally published in Great Britain by J.M. Dent & Sons Ltd.

PRINTING HISTORY

J.M. Dent edition published 1985
Corgi edition published 1988

This book is set in 11/12 pt Century Textbook
by Colset Private Limited, Singapore.

Corgi Books are published by Transworld Publishers Ltd., 61–63 Uxbridge Road, Ealing, London W5 5SA, in Australia by Transworld Publishers (Australia) Pty. Ltd., 15–23 Helles Avenue, Moorebank, NSW 2170, and in New Zealand by Transworld Publishers (N.Z.) Ltd., Cnr. Moselle and Waipareira Avenues, Henderson, Auckland.

Made and printed in Great Britain by
Cox & Wyman Ltd., Reading, Berks.

For William, Martin and Harry

Men-a-vaur

Kettle Rocks

ST HEL

Shipman Head

Gun
Hole

Pipers
Hole

Hangmans
Island

Old
Grim

New
Grimsby

BRYHER

Plumb
Island

TRES

Carn Near

SAMSON

THE

~St

Har

Star
Castle

ST MARY

ANNET

GUGH

ST AGNES

Western Rocks

Bishop Rock
●

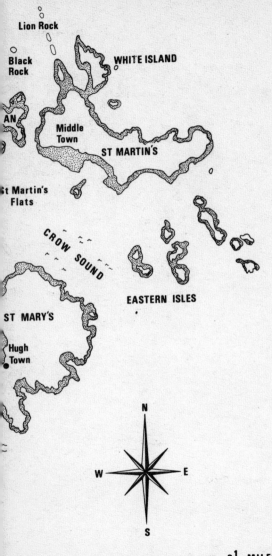

Lion Rock

Black
Rock

WHITE ISLAND

AN

Middle
Town

ST MARTIN'S

St Martin's
Flats

CROW ~ ~
~
SOUND ~ ~ ~

EASTERN ISLES

ST MARY'S

Hugh
Town

N

W    E

S

2½ MILES

# 1

The kitchen was small and very hot. It seemed even hotter than it was because it was full of smoke from two mackerel in the frying pan on the gas stove. The old radio on the shelf was tuned to Radio 2, and the presenter was saying something that might have been funny if it had been audible above the shrill yelling of the old woman. She was swearing at the cat because it had just tried to fish a mackerel out of the pan, burned its paw and leaped on to a high shelf where it had spilt the tea caddy into the milk jug. The old woman, who was called Grannie Dole, was purplish with rage.

The thin boy prodding the mackerel with an old tin fork kept quiet. He had lived with Grannie Dole long enough to know what you did when. Just now, you cooked the breakfast while Grannie had it out with Mr Wilson the cat, and you ate it as fast as you could. Then you hopped it like a streak of lightning before Grannie Dole asked if you had done your homework. Grannie Dole didn't have much clue about homework, not knowing how to read. But she took her responsibilities as Gussie's guardian seriously, when she remembered.

Gussie groaned at the mackerel. It was another

Monday morning, and he was in another impossible situation. It was now six o'clock, and the boat that took the Tresco children cross-channel to St Mary's Comprehensive left at nine. On Saturday night, Grannie Dole had had one of her turns and drunk up the Social Security money. This meant she would not eat anything until next S.S. day, unless Gussie got her some money within the next three hours. Gussie had been putting off doing his homework, saving it for the last minute. So now he had a straight choice. Either he kept Grannie Dole going by earning her some money for food, or he did his homework and kept Mr Hulbert happy. Mr Hulbert was the English master, and a good bloke. Gussie did not like to let him down. But if he didn't do his stuff, Grannie would starve. Mr Hulbert, Gussie decided, would probably live. He sighed. Then he pulled on his jersey. Grannie Dole seemed to be concentrating on keeping Mr Wilson in a Jap stranglehold. He sidled out of the door.

The road ran along the shore here. Across five miles of cement-coloured water the Western Rocks were a tangle of grey sea and white foam in the cold light of dawn. The Isles of Scilly are off the end of Cornwall, and the waves that hit them are enormous because they have travelled all the way from Canada, driven by the west wind. The wind cut through Gussie's jersey and he shoved his hands in his pockets to ward off the chill. His right hand met crumpled paper, and he groaned again. Sometimes he felt completely fed-up with Grannie Dole. He pulled out the letter. Welfare Snell had given it to him on St Mary's Quay on Friday night.

Dear Mrs Woodcock, (*this was Grannie Dole's real name. Nobody used it, except Snell*)

I regret to inform you that it has come to my notice that your ward, Augustus Smith, has been absent from school two days this week. He offers no excuse except that he had 'work to do'. Since these days bring the total of his non-attendance to twenty-six days this term, I and my colleagues in the relevant Authorities feel that the time has come for action, in the boy's interests. I must therefore inform you that if there is any repetition of this truancy, the County Care authorities will exercise the options open to them.

Yours faithfully,<br>
Q. B. Snell, Welfare Officer.

It was the last sentence that gave Gussie the chills.

Welfare Snell had shiny black hair and horn-rimmed glasses. He had come from the Mainland. He hated Scilly, and his first name was Quentin. He liked everything to be nice and regular. The first time Gussie had played truant, Snell had asked him why he hadn't been at school. Gussie, who had been setting lobster pots from his old boat, had said truthfully he'd forgotten. Snell had hated him ever since.

Gussie's parents were dead. But he had an Uncle Guy in Plymouth, who sold second-hand cars and wore shiny suits. When Uncle Guy came to Scilly, his little moustache always writhed under his long nose. It writhed at the salt that got on his shiny black shoes, the tiny roads that made it necessary for him to leave his Ford

Granada on the mainland, at the piles of wreck-wood that took the place of the central heating tank behind Grannie Dole's cottage. Gussie felt a sort of duty to him because he was his uncle. But it was the kind of duty he would have felt towards a wax model of a policeman.

Uncle Guy was the option open to Snell. Gussie did not want to go to Plymouth, not only because he hated the place but because without him, Welfare Snell would put Grannie Dole in Bide-a-Wee, the old folk's home on St Mary's. And if ever she went there, she had promised to go on permanent hunger-strike. Gussie knew that she meant it. Grannie Dole was tough; Mr Wilson the cat was going to have a stiff neck for weeks.

Down at the beach, the tide was going out, the sand grey in front of the wet palm trees. Gussie climbed into the old boat. There was no diesel for the engine so he pulled up the mooring, unsnapped the painter from the buoyrope, unshipped the oars and began to row across the channel towards the square little fields on Bryher. The wind cleaned away the pan grease stuck in his throat, and he began to feel that he was his own boss again. The boat always made him feel that. Catch Welfare Snell out in a rowing boat. Hah!

Dark was waiting for him on the beach at Bryher. He scrambled in over the side, swearing a bit when his feet got wet. He was fourteen to Gussie's thirteen, but much smaller. Gussie was tall and lanky and had hair the colour of old rope. Dark was solid and square and scowled a good deal. He reckoned that one of his great-grandfathers must have been a Spaniard washed off a ship near Bryher – or even something to do with the Spanish Armada. Some of the Armada ships had come ashore at Scilly, so people said.

Now, Dark hunched into his old anorak as the boat inched up the channel towards the grey slot of open sea. He ran his eyes over the sleek sixty-foot motor yacht anchored between the islands. '*Good Impression*,' he said. 'Funny name for a boat. Sell them some eggs, maybe.'

'No,' said Gussie. 'Birdwatchers. You remember when we tried to sell eggs to them bird-watchers larse year?'

Dark nodded briefly. He remembered, all right.

'Police and everything,' said Gussie. 'Island 'otel will have 'em, though.'

'Nice boat,' said Dark.

'Ah,' said Gussie, absentmindedly. He didn't much care about the yachts that came and anchored between the islands. The blokes off them went to the pub and bought stuff at the shop, and then went up to look at the Abbey gardens. He didn't do any of that himself. He was too busy working for a living.

He pulled between the granite headlands, past a castle with a tower that looked like a granite oil drum. At the mouth of the harbour the swell began to lift the boat, and they moved into the open sea.

Half an hour later they were under Men-a-Vaur.

Men-a-Vaur is a rock that looks like the dorsal fins of three fish, swimming side by side. Its three blades are perhaps eighty feet high; they stand in deep water, and the Atlantic surges through the channels between them like black ink. Gussie said, 'My turn to go.'

13

Dark started to protest but Gussie was already handing over the oars, and it was stupid to mess about in a boat on a big sea. Besides, Gussie was right. Gussie was always right, except that he was right in a different way from other people. Dark saw no harm in being wrong himself, as long as he wasn't found out.

The swells were very big where they were. In the troughs it was like being at the bottom of a small valley. When the wave rolled under, it seemed impossibly steep, as if the boat would fall off the slope and roll into the bottom. And once on top, for a moment you felt higher than the gulls and could see Round Island and the Golden Ball and the Kettle spewing foam a hundred feet in the air – the top was the worst of the lot.

But Dark knew all about waves, or he pretended he did when he was with Gussie. So he pulled down the tide to the high, grey blades of Men-a-Vaur. And in ten minutes their shadow was blotting out the sun, and his stomach felt hollow and empty when he caught the draw and suck of the waves around the rocks. But he went in, because of Gussie. He went in stern first, down a little lane of black water in the white foam. Then he waited, twenty feet off the rock, until he felt the new wave swelling under the keel, and Gussie said, 'Now!' and he gave a final shove at the oars and Gussie stepped on to a ledge at the top of the wave and Dark pulled hard. Five seconds later he was twenty yards away, giggling with relief. And Gussie was climbing – pale and spidery – up the white-streaked granite with gulls diving at his head.

The white streaks were gulls' muck and they stank. Gussie screwed up his nose and breathed through his mouth. He climbed very carefully, feeling with his toes for the little notches and crannies in the rock. The wind fluttered the loose threads of his jersey and shoved at the straw shopping bag slung over his shoulder. He paused, looking up. The rock was a great arrowhead reeling against the scudding clouds. He climbed on, buffeted by the downdraught from the screaming herring gulls.

Halfway up the rock, a ledge ran at a shallow angle across the face. Gussie pulled himself on to it and sat back. Below, a colony of kittiwakes clustered round the steep crack where they laid their eggs. The eggs were conical, so if they rolled they rolled in a tight circle. Herring gulls preferred flatter ground. Gussie knew all about gulls. The nests were piles of rubbish among the little green cushions of sea-pinks that somehow eked a living up here. He took an egg from each, two from nests with four eggs. Those he did not take he marked with a Magic Marker he had swiped from old Hulbert's desk at school, so he would know not to take them next time he came.

When he had finished with the ledge he climbed up to the spine of the rock. The wind was much stronger up here. It flattened his hair on his head and pulled his eyes out of shape so they watered. There were no nests. Even gulls like a bit of shelter. Far below, Dark and the boat were as tiny as a willow-leaf on the indigo sea. The sun had come out and beyond the streaks of foam from the Golden Ball bar, Tresco was green with shooting heather.

A man was walking round the cliff path from the direction of New Grimsby Harbour. He was half a mile away, but Scilly air is clear and Gussie's eyes were as sharp as a gull's. The man was short and fat – Gussie didn't recognize him. There was something funny about the way he walked: as if one of his knees were stiff, thought Gussie. No, that wasn't it. He frowned, and kept watching. Gussie liked solving mysteries.

The man came closer. He limped down on to the rocks beside the dark mouth of Piper's Hole. As sometimes happens, the sea had fallen quiet. He limped down the huge, sloping slab of granite and stood looking north towards a group of fishing-boats bobbing close to the horizon. Mackerel boats, thought Gussie; it was the time of year. Then he looked back at the man, and his mouth opened to shout. But no shout came, only the sound of the wind howling in his teeth . . . because there was a huge wave towering over him. The man had seen it. Gussie watched him lurch back, his arms waving like little windmills. Then his leg caught in a crack and over he went, and the wave licked up the slab like a big, white tongue of foam

16

and covered him. And when the wave went back the slab was empty.

Gussie started shaking so much he thought he would fall off. But when he looked down Dark was there, and he hadn't seen anything. (Trust Dark to keep his eyes shut.) And when Gussie looked back at Tresco there was a little black head in the waves off Piper's Hole. A head that might have been a seal's, except that seals do not have arms that flail the water. The head vanished. Oh lor, thought Gussie, and felt himself starting to shake again. The head reappeared. And next time's the third time, Gussie thought, and found himself shouting words that the wind grabbed and tore away. The head went under again.

Very cautiously, Gussie started the long climb down. He had a strange, empty feeling; he knew that what he had just seen had happened, but he could not quite believe it.

The head came up again. This time it bobbed well out of the water, the shoulders, too. The man must be a very strong swimmer. He held his breath as the head and upper torso bobbed towards the same tilted slab it had been washed off two minutes before. Another wave came, tumbling white. The man went with it. When the wave receded, he was still there, crawling like a fly.

Gussie cheered. Then his heart seemed to roll over in his chest, and his skin prickled horribly.

*One of the man's legs was gone.*

Horror froze him to the rocks. A few years previously, a man had been walking on that same rock, and a wave had grabbed him. The next wave had put him back – without his hands. Gussie half-slid the rest of the way down the ledge, scarcely noticing the void beneath him. At the ledge he looked again.

The man was on his feet – foot. He had found a long bit of driftwood to use as a crutch, and he was hopping up the rocks at great speed. Gussie had never lost a leg himself and did not know anyone who had, but he was pretty sure that he wouldn't be hopping about like a heron three minutes after he'd lost it. There'd be blood, too. The man was wearing blue and yellow striped underpants. There was no blood.

'Cor,' said Gussie. The limp. The struggle in the sea. It all clicked into place.

The man hopped over the hill. Gussie shouldered the straw bag of eggs and slithered down the rock. Dark came in to fetch him. He was sweating a bit; Dark hated Men-a-Vaur.

As Gussie stepped on to the after-thwart a freak wave side-slapped the boat. He stumbled and would have fallen if he had not grabbed at the gunwale. The straw bag hit the bottom-boards with a crunch.

'Look out!' said Dark.

Gussie did not seem to have noticed. 'Did you see that?' he said.

'Course I did. Clumsy idjit.'

'Not that. The other thing.'

'What other thing? Look, mate, I thought you wanted to sell them eggs?'

'Never mind the eggs,' said Gussie. He rummaged through a locker and pulled out a coil of line and a small grappling iron. 'It's legs I'm after.'

'Legs?'

'Things above your feet,' said Gussie. 'Gimme those oars.'

# 2

Palace Row is a concrete lane, just wide enough for a tractor, that runs down to New Grimsby Quay. An hour later Gussie and Dark were strolling along it, whistling. Gussie had a foot in his hand. Dark had a thigh. Between the foot and thigh were two-feet six-inches of aluminium artificial leg, wearing a brown sock with a parrot on it. They would have left it on the yacht, but the yacht was gone and Gussie was just about sure the birdwatchers would be pestering terns on Annet, out towards the Bishop Rock.

Short Henry Pender was leaning on his garden wall, smoking a fag and watching the harbour. He said, 'Cor. What you got there, boys?'

'What's it look like?' said Gussie.

There was a roar from behind them. Someone shouted, 'My leg!' And from out of the Quay Shop hopped the fat man. He was using a shrimping net as a crutch and wearing one of Mrs Oglander's SCILLY ME t-shirts over his blue and yellow underpants. Dark snorted with laughter.

Gussie said, 'Yours is it? We fished 'er up for you.'

'Blast you,' yelled the man. 'Blast you!' He had very black hair and very red skin, and his eyebrows met over his short shiny nose. 'I have had the most appalling walk. Beastly time. Give it back, blast you!' He snatched it out of Gussie's hands. Instead of putting it back on, he pulled down the sock, opened a little sliding door, and looked into a compartment. Then he shouted so loudly that seagulls flapped squawking from the quay-shop roof. 'GONE!' he roared. 'Have you taken it, you pestilential brats?'

'Taken what?' said Dark. The one-legged man sat down on the low granite wall and shoved his stump (it looked a bit like a baby's head) into the socket at the top of the leg.

'Tape recorder,' said the man. 'All wrapped up in polythene. I kept it in me leg because it . . . No damn business of yours *why* I kept it there.'

'Must of fell out,' said Dark. Gussie noticed that Dark was doing his Invisible Retreat steps, appearing to shift from foot to foot but actually reversing out of range at goodish speed. There was a bulge in his pocket where there had been none before. Gussie grinned sheepishly at the one-legged man and set off in pursuit.

He caught Dark at the end of the quay. The school boat was alongside, the boys and girls swinging their week's luggage and wishing they could stay on Tresco without having to weekly-board on St Mary's.

'You nicked his tape recorder,' said Gussie.

Dark's black eyes shifted away. 'So?'

'Poor bloke's only got one leg. Give it back.'

'He's got one leg. I've got no tape recorder.'

'Thief.'

'Nah.' Dark wiped his nose with an air of finality. 'Salvage. You want your share. You'll get it.'

'Nope,' said Gussie.

Dark leered at him in a peculiarly irritating way, and said, 'You'd better tell 'im, then. I'm off to school.'

Gussie realized with a shock that the boat was ready to leave and that he didn't have his boarder's bag. He rushed round the harbour, feet slapping on the road, and up to his room. There he picked up his bag and began running back. As he rounded the hedge he could see Snidger Jenkins, the school boatman, casting off the bowline. He spurted. But as he was dashing past Mrs Emmett's house at the corner of Palace Row, a hand came out and gripped him firmly by the shoulder.

'Ow,' said Gussie, wriggling. The fingers were like iron bars. 'Leggo.'

'I want a word,' said the one-legged man.

'I got to go,' said Gussie. Short Henry was casting off astern; white foam bubbled under the school boat's counter.

'I want my tape recorder,' said the one-legged man. 'I'll pay.'

'I haven't got it,' said Gussie. 'Honest. Please, I've got to go to school.'

'You should have thought of that when you pinched my tape recorder,' said Pegleg. Gussie wrenched away, but Pegleg's grip remained vice-like.

'*Please*,' said Gussie. But it was too late already.

There was green water between the school boat and the quay now. Dark waved from the stern. Pegleg let go, seeming to relent. Gussie's head dropped and he plunged his hands in his pockets.

He'd had it.

'You haven't got it, I haven't got it, your friend hasn't got it,' said the one-legged man in a kindlier tone. 'It must be on the bottom of the sea. Let's go and look.'

Gussie shook his head miserably.

'I'll pay you ten pounds.'

The gulls' eggs were broken, and Grannie Dole had no money. Ten pounds was a lot of money. Ought he to tell on Dark, or take this bloke's money under false pretences? Dark was his mate. Gussie cursed Dark silently for doing this to him. Then he jerked his head towards his boat and said, 'Let's go.'

As he pulled towards Piper's Hole, he worked out what he'd do. He'd pretend to look for half-an-hour, then row over to St Mary's, perhaps get a tow. That way he'd only be late for school, not absent. But the one-legged man did not see it like that. He insisted on searching every nook and cranny and even on grappling, though Gussie told him it was useless to grapple for something small and square.

The one-legged man said his name was Hopcraft. At first he talked a lot. The yacht *Good Impression* contained the Civil Service Birdwatchers' Club, he said. He was very interested in birds, particularly Arctic terns. He explained to Gussie that they migrated annually from the Arctic to the Antarctic. Gussie grunted politely. He knew about Arctic terns already. His mind was on other things. At eleven o'clock he said, 'Tide's turned. We'll never find it now.'

Hopcraft had been rather silent for ten minutes or so, scrabbling under lumps of granite with a stick. 'We've got to find it,' he said.

'Need a diver, then.'

Hopcraft's rather bulging eyes stuck out of his head.

'Ah!' he said. 'A diver! Where can I get a diver?'

'St Mary's,' said Gussie. 'We'd better go now. I'm late.'

'No, we'll have a last look.' Pegleg said it as if he was used to bossing people about. Gussie contained himself for five minutes. It was twenty-past eleven. It'd take at least an hour to get to St Mary's. It was too late to bother. Gritting his teeth, Gussie shoved Snell's letter firmly out of his mind. He said, 'Let's go,' and started to row. Back at the quay Hopcraft struggled out of the boat. At the top of the steps he gave Gussie two fivers. They were soggy and he looked tired. Gussie felt suddenly sorry for him. He trotted back to the house and gave the money to Grannie Dole. She said, 'Shun't you be at school?'

Gussie said, 'Yes, Gran,' not moving his lips. Grannie Dole was deaf, but pretended not to be. 'Ah, orright,' she said. 'Just so long as.' Then he set off to see Maurice Tanner.

23

The road ran along the side of Abbey Hill, between dark forests of rhododendron and Monterey pine. Through gaps in the trees, a grey lake appeared. Ordinarily Gussie would have paused to eye the rafts of water-fowl floating among the reed beds, for it was a famous stopping-off point for migrating birds, and rarities were almost commonplace. But today he trudged up the road with his eyes on his feet, weighed down with impending doom.

Maurice Tanner lived in a shed behind a cloister to whose pillars were bolted the brilliantly coloured figureheads of sailing ships wrecked at Scilly in what were generally known as the Bad Old Days (though Gussie couldn't see much wrong with them himself). Maurice had been a gardener in the island's thirty acres of rare plants, until a tree had fallen on him and he had lost the use of his legs. Now he sat in his shed and did things with his musical instruments and his computer and his radio ham set, resisting all attempts to move him to somewhere on the mainland with Facilities for the Disabled. Gussie was threading through the ferns towards the hut door when a giant voice boomed, 'WHAT ARE YOU DOING OFF SCHOOL, GUSSIE SMITH?' Gussie jumped a foot in the air. 'COME ON IN YOU LITTLE PERISHER,' said the voice. Gussie recognized it as Maurice's. He went in.

The shed was lined with books, except on one wall where green light from a computer's VDU glittered on the glass front of a musical-instrument cabinet. Beside the computer was the ham radio set. A light hiss of static filled the room.

'How'd you know it was me?' said Gussie.

'Magic,' said Maurice, with a flash of white teeth. 'TV magic. Put a camera in a tree, wired it to the screen. Speaker above the door. Built a new amplifier. Look.' His tattooed arms grasped a set of the bars that criss-crossed the shed at head height, and he swung across to a cabinet, legs trailing behind him. 'Nice, innit?'

Gussie admired Maurice's workmanship. The printed circuits looked like jewellery; Maurice was a huge man, but his fingers did neat, meticulous things. He swung back. 'Well?' he said. The light from the TV screen twinkled in his gold earrings, but he did not sound cheerful. His blue eyes were less friendly than usual.

'Well?' he said again. 'Why not at school?'

Gussie shrugged. Maurice sighed, adjusted a spotlight, and returned to his work. It was his habit, while working, to explain what he was doing.

'Little tape recorder,' said Maurice. 'Your mate Dark brought it in to me. *He* went to school, this morning. Mrs Potterton was ill so they had a free period, so he hitched a lift back with Snidger and came to show me this here tape machine because it's making a funny noise. I had a look at it and I'm surprised it wasn't blowing bubbles. There was about a pint of seawater in it.

'So out comes the water and I'll just take it to bits and splosh it in this bowl of fresh water, to get the salt off before I put it back together. Nice machine. I didn't know Dark was interested in birdwatching.'

It took Gussie a moment to catch up. 'He's not,' he said.

'Well, the tape was full of birdwatching notes.' Maurice dabbed the capstans of the cassette recorder with a tiny paintbrush. 'Actually, I sort of wonder where he got it from,' he said. 'Expensive machine.'

'Dunno.' Gussie wished he could tell the truth. But he couldn't. Maurice looked at him sharply, saw freckled jaws clamped tight, eyes shadowed in deep sockets.

'He'll tell us, no doubt,' said Maurice. 'Now make us some coffee and explain why you aren't at school.'

Gussie made coffee, with sweetened condensed milk for him and rum for Maurice. Then he attempted an explanation. There wasn't one, and he was a hopeless liar, so it wasn't easy. 'Had to help Grannie Dole,' he said. 'Didn't have time for school.'

Maurice sighed. 'They won't like that, Gus. You know what they'll say. Grannie Dole must help herself, or go to Bide-a-Wee. And as for you . . .'

Gussie passed him Snell's letter. Maurice's lips moved as he read it; the words might have been, 'Shiny-haired creep,' but you couldn't be sure. At the end, he sighed. 'Well,' he said. 'James Hulbert owes me a favour.'

Hulbert, the English teacher, was a friend of Maurice's. This was a bit of luck for Gussie. He was the first to admit that he didn't come across too well at school. It wasn't that he didn't *like* school, it was just that it didn't seem to have much to do with real life. What good would irregular verbs be when you were heaving lobster pots about? Thanks to Maurice, Gussie was pretty good on the computer, and he read a lot of books. But at school there were queues for the computer, and the books were a bit, well, childish.

Gussie had finally come to the conclusion that school was all very well for stopping blokes frittering their time away, but it was not much use to anyone who was serious about life, like he was. Maurice understood this, and in the past he had managed to make Hulbert understand it too.

'Okay,' said Maurice. 'I'll ring him, and he'll do his best. But you want to watch out for Snell. He doesn't, er, understand.'

'Snell's a shiny-haired creep,' said Gussie.

'Show some respect, brat,' said Maurice, dialling. 'And wait outside while I talk.'

Gussie could hear Maurice's voice, mumbling. It seemed to go on for a long time. Eventually, the phone clicked down and the huge voice boomed from the hidden speakers. 'YOU ARE FORGIVEN. NOW COME IN HERE.'

They spent the rest of the day on Maurice's computer. He had invented a game called Snells and Crocs, in which tiny Snells swam across rivers full of crocodiles. The way the program worked it was impossible for the Snells to get through. It was just about Gussie's favourite game.

Much later, Gussie was walking through the gardens. The wind was rustling the leaves of the royal palms, and the air smelt of aromatic plants. He was feeling good; old Maurice was great. He'd really sorted things out. He was whistling as he went through the granite arch and down the drive, under the dark shadows of the ilex trees. Now all he had to do was tell Dark what he thought of him, for making him miss school . . .

A violent pain grew in his left ear, and a thin, harsh voice said, 'Gussie Smith. Whisssstling, are you? The merry truant, is it? We'll see what the mainland will do for you.'

27

The face was long and pale, with horn-rimmed spectacles behind which little eyes glittered with mean glee. Gussie could smell the grease plastering the black hair to the skull. He said, 'But Mr Hulbert said . . .'

'I don't care what Mr Hulbert said,' hissed the thin mouth. 'Now you come back to your gran's and we'll talk, and then we'll arrange for you to go to your Uncle Guy's.'

'You can't do that,' said Gussie. 'I've just come from Maurice Tanner and he rang up Mr Hulbert and Mr Hulbert said he's fixed everything . . .'

'Oh,' said the thin voice. 'So Mr Hulbert's the Welfare Officer now, is he? We'll have to see about this. But of course it's no concern of yours, because you're coming back to your horrible little house and we're going to have a good long talk about your, er, future. Yours and your gran's.'

'You leave Grannie out of this.'

'Sssssilence, child,' hissed the voice. 'You will find that the real world is a complicated place.' There was a shifty look in his eye, as if he were treading on difficult ground. 'All you have to know is that what I and the Committee say, goes.' The thumb and forefinger tightened triumphantly on Gussie's ear. Rocks, sea and sky spun round his head. 'You and your grannie are both in this together. In need of care and special vigilance. You to Plymouth, her to the Home. Clear cut and cut and dried. Very sad. Oh, *very* sad,' said Welfare Snell.

## 3

As they opened the door of the house, the smoke came out to meet them. Living with Grannie Dole, Gussie had grown to know smoke pretty well. Gussie noted automatically that this was beef stew smoke with a hint of potato. The Snell shoved him roughly into the room and stood peering through the murk. Gussie knew that the smoke was usually thinnest near the floor, so he bent double, crept across to the stove and turned off the gas. Snell was saying, 'Mrs Woodcock!' and breaking down in coughing fits. Gussie opened a window, and the smoke billowed over the small, wild garden and the horseshoe of the harbour. Its disappearance revealed Mr Wilson the cat perched on a high shelf, and in the corner Grannie Dole, rusty black. Only her eyes moved, small, blue, and bloodshot. Gussie noticed with a sinking heart that there was a half-empty bottle of gin on the table beside her.

'Augustus!' she cried. '*And* Mr Snell! Oh, Augustus, how could you do this to me?'

'Do what?' said Gussie.

'Eeeek!' shrieked Grannie. She was in one of her real rages, thought Gussie miserably. 'Mr Snell tells me that you wasn't on the school boat 'smorning for no good reason! That you been

29

lollygagging and gallivanting and mucking about when you should have been, well, at school. Consider the beneficiousness of a good education, Gussie! The wonderful chance they gives you to get ahead in the world! To learn how to get the engine going on that old boat of yourn. All, all,' said Grannie, remembering some holy tract from her deep past, 'is knowledge. But what do you do? You goes off playing and cheeking and who knows what all!' Gussie knew she had to go until she ran down, so he fixed his eyes on Mr Wilson, teetering on a pile of tobacco tins above the fuming saucepan.

'I mind the day, mind it well, when your mum and dad went off. "Mind th' baby," they said to me, you being six months. And then the wind come up and your mum and dad went down, put by a wave on to the Crim and no survivors, and there you was, a puking nipper with a pore, tired old woman. But I dragged you up, Master Gussie. Oh I dragged you up through thick, thin and gorse bushes, and what thanks do I get? Pore Mr Snell has to come over from St Mary's and tell me you bin missing school and he has got, much against his will, to take you to Plymouth and me to the HOME!'

Grannie Dole uttered the last word in a ginny shriek that made Mr Wilson jump as if scalded. The pile of tobacco tins disintegrated. The cat fell into the stew, leaped out and exited screeching through the window.

'I'LL GET YOU FOR THAT!' roared Grannie Dole. 'ME LOVELY BEEF STEW!'

Then, remembering that she was doing her Pore Old Woman bit, 'Oh, a sore trial, Mr Snell. We slaves and slaves to keep respectable, but

30

what does we get? Ingratitude.' She turned her face to Gussie. The eye Snell could not see winked, hard.

Gussie winked back but he knew it was too late for winking. 'I was up at Maurice's,' he said. 'We rung Mr Hulbert. We were working on Maurice's computer. Mr Hulbert said everything was okay so long as I came to school tomorrow.'

'Mr Hulbert has no authority to make conditions of this kind,' said Snell in a voice like cold porridge. 'I am the Welfare Officer, and I make the decisions.'

Gussie went chilly all over. 'But Mr Hulbert and Maurice agreed . . .'

Snell smiled, lowering his pale eyelids. 'I fear we cannot take into account the ideas of every Tom, Dick and Harry. Our job is to keep the pupils at the school. It is all part of the way we look after people.'

'But Mr Hulbert . . .'

'Mr Hulbert does not concern me.' Snell's eyes darted across to Grannie Dole. 'Even if I thought you were telling the truth about what he said.' From past experience Snell knew that Gussie and Grannie Dole trusted each other. He wanted to break that down, too.

But Grannie Dole had been watching him closely, and she wasn't having any of that. 'As for *you*, you slimy-'aired weasel, knockin' your way in on people and telling them what's for their own good! When you're a wossling foreigner as doesn't know how we conducts our lives here and always has . . .'

'We live in a changing world,' said Snell primly.

'*Doan you contradict me!*' roared Grannie Dole, with a huge gesture of her arm that knocked over the gin bottle. 'OO do you think you *are*? What business is it of yourn what we do?'

Welfare Snell was looking uncomfortable. He shifted from foot to foot and accidentally trod on Mr Wilson who had licked the burnt beef stew off his paws and crept back to look for more. 'KEEEECCCHHH!' cried Mr Wilson.

'Come in here and damage my cat, would you!' shrieked Grannie Dole. Gussie couldn't help laughing at Snell's discomfiture. Snell saw the corners of his mouth twitch and went pale with rage.

'I'll see you're dealt with,' said Snell. '*Thoroughly* dealt with.' Gussie didn't feel like laughing any more. 'You've got a day to pack. Leaving for Plymouth on the Wednesday afternoon chopper. And perhaps Mrs Woodcock would be ready at that time to come to the Bide-a-Wee Home?' Snell placed a brown envelope tenderly on the table. 'You will find the relevant papers in here. Care Order confirmation and so on. It is all *official* now. You understand?' He turned towards the door.

At that moment, someone knocked, hard. The door opened, and round it appeared the bulging, red face of Mr Hopcraft, of the Civil Service Birdwatchers' Club.

'Hello,' said Hopcraft. 'Sorry to butt in but I was wondering if you're free tomorrow? The other chaps are going to look at the terns again, but I'm not too keen on terns. Prefer kittiwakes; kittiwakes nest on rocks. I wanted to hire you to take me round those rocks to the north.' He gestured with thick fingers vaguely northwards. 'Watch kittiwakes nesting.'

Gussie opened his mouth to refuse. But Snell said, 'I'm afraid that will be impossible. Augustus will be leaving the Islands the day after tomorrow. As Welfare Officer on the case . . .'

'Wednesday?' said Pegleg. Something happened to him; his cheeks were puffing, his eyes slitting, and he came up on his toes like a boxer. 'Tomorrow's Tuesday, is it not? I fail to see that even a social worker can change that.'

'I am a Welfare Officer,' said Snell.

'Ah,' said Pegleg. To Gussie's delight he bowed deeply from the waist. 'I *do* apologize. As a mere Permanent Under-Secretary at the Department, I had not realized that Welfare Officers were now at liberty to tamper with the calendar . . .'

Snell turned a nasty colour. His mouth opened and shut like a cod's.

'What does be going on?' said Grannie Dole. 'What you talking about?'

33

'I apologize,' said Pegleg, with another bow. 'I was simply asking if Gussie could take me out in the boat in the morning.' His eyes, bulging and glittering, looked at Gussie. 'Or perhaps you're busy?'

'No,' said Gussie. He could feel Snell boiling like a kettle, and he spoke slowly to prolong the delightful moment. 'I don't believe I'm doing anything. I'll pick you up at nine, off the yacht.'

'Nine it is,' said Pegleg. 'Mrs Woodcock, goodbye, and Welfare Officer, er, didn't catch your name.'

He was gone before Snell could enlighten him.

But funnily enough the Snell that walked down towards the quay was not an unhappy Snell. In fact, he was a Snell whose hands curled with silent glee, and whose mouth twisted with secret mirth under his long and inquisitive nose. Snell loved order, precision, and long forms correctly filled in. He worshipped a god who accepted sacrifices of typed paper made by priests who spoke an Official Secret Language, and did miracles by which rules, already made, multiplied amazingly. Snell looked forward to a day when there would be rules to govern eating, sleeping and breathing. But where Gussie Smith was concerned, he was ready to bend the rules a little. He had bent them tonight, just enough.

For Gussie Smith was a creature of the old world. He was honest and straightforward, and he seemed to love Grannie Dole and want to look after her. But of course he was under age. Looking after the elderly was not Gussie's job – was, indeed, against the rules.

Snell hated Gussie Smith with a hatred that much resembled fear.

After Snell had gone, Grannie Dole rubbed her hands, looked with regret at the spilt gin bottle, and dished out stew. Gussie ate it automatically. It might as well have been coal. Actually it bore a strong resemblance to coal, being black and crunchy. But he was thinking about Snell and Grannie and what was going to happen on Wednesday. He reckoned nobody could stop old Snell. Snell was on top. Trouble was that Grannie Dole wasn't his real guardian; Uncle Guy was. The thought of Uncle Guy was too much. He got up and said, 'I'm going for a walk.'

'That's right,' said Grannie Dole. But he could see she was worried now. 'Doan you worry. We'll fix 'em.' They grinned at each other, though neither of them felt at all like grinning. Gussie ripped open Snell's envelope and ran an eye over the contents. There was a letter headed INTERIM PROVISION OF CARE. Gussie read no further.

It was a soft night, with a drift of rain and a strong smell of salted mackerel from the bait shed. Gussie went down to the beach and looked at his boat. He wouldn't be able to take her to Plymouth. Unfair, thought Gussie. Grannie Dole would have said it was enough to make you weep. Gussie did not weep. All he wanted was to scupper Snell. But how?

''Ullo Gussie,' said Dark's voice. 'What's 'appening?'

Gussie was in no mood to talk to Dark who had caused all this trouble. But he said, 'Why aren't you at school, idiot face?'

'I was. I got a lift back with Humphrey Atkins in the oil boat.'

'What happened?'

'They asked where you were. Partickerly Hulbert. He's all right, old Hulbert.'

'Yeah,' said Gussie. He had no desire to explain his day to Dark.

'You coming tomorrow?'

'No,' said Gussie shortly. Then, returning to the root cause of the trouble, he said, 'Got your recorder back?'

'Maurice wants it to dry out.'

'Didn't know you were keen on birdwatching.'

Dark laughed his cunning laugh. 'That was the tape come with it. All about roseate terns in Shropshire.'

'Funny,' said Gussie. 'Shropshire's miles from the sea, and you only see 'em on the coast.'

'Prob'ly mad ones,' said Dark. 'Had a bit of a tern.' He began to laugh in a manner that Gussie found intensely irritating. Gussie got up and walked away. Dark followed him. 'Sorry,' Dark said in a new voice. 'I s'pose it's all my fault, innit? But . . . well, once I'd nicked it I couldn't give it back. Could I? I mean they would have known. I'll make it up to you, though. Gussie?'

But Gussie had walked away, and Dark's voice was thin and faint in the wind and slanting rain. As he hunched his shoulders and screwed up his eyes, he heard Dark's voice again, thin as a seagull's cry.

'Anyway it was salvage, Gussie. Salvaaage!'

Gussie walked on.

Gussie's room was low, with a sloping roof that meant he had to walk on his hands and knees under the eaves. On the walls were wreck pictures from

36

Gibson's, huge sailing ships covered in boiling waves, sails shredded. There were also pictures Maurice had given him of cars. Gussie didn't see many cars, since there were none on Tresco and the ones on St Mary's tended to fall to bits because of the steep, narrow roads and the salt in the air. The tiny window let in a thin, grey light; outside, the wind buffeted the slates.

When Gussie awoke, he lay wondering why he felt hollow, as if he were hungry and frightened at the same time. Then he remembered. He pulled on his clothes and padded to the kitchen. He made himself a marmalade sandwich, drank a glass of water, and trudged off to the beach. The clouds were high, and the last of the dawn was still yellowing the eastern sky. Gulls shrieked, and the water smacked loudly at the boats moored in the harbour. Plymouth was not going to be like this.

He pulled a tiny dinghy down the beach, shipped the oars and rowed out to his boat. When he had made fast he climbed aboard and sat on the thwart, resplicing a buoy rope. While his fingers worked at the blue rope he wished he didn't have to take Pegleg on a trip. If it was his last day on Scilly, he wanted to spend it by himself. But he had agreed. Mostly out of thankfulness at the way Pegleg had squashed Snell, it was true. And an agreement was an agreement.

At eight, he unsnapped the mooring shackle and rowed out to the yacht. A couple of men in white yachting caps were standing by her wheelhouse smoking cigarettes and looking miserable in the wind. They stared at Gussie as he came alongside. 'Is Mr Hopcraft ready?' he asked.

'Ah, I really couldn't say,' said one of them. 'It is possible.'

'Well, yes and no,' said the other one. 'Hard to be certain.'

'Could you give him a shout, please?' said Gussie politely.

Their eyebrows shot up until they were invisible under the peaks of their yachting caps.

'A *shout*?' said the first one. 'Can you, ah, *shout*, Cedric?'

'I don't believe I have ever tried,' said Cedric. He cleared his throat and mewed, 'Pegleg! PEGLEG!'

Hopcroft appeared on deck, purple in the face, and munching toast. 'Ah! Fine. Excellent!' he cried, brandishing the toast. 'Good Lord, are we going to row all the way?'

'No diesel,' said Gussie.

'We'll get some,' said Pegleg, and began issuing long strings of orders. A man in a dirty singlet came on deck, took Gussie's can, and filled it. Gussie glugged it into the tank. The engine started, its heavy chug releasing a satisfying volume of black smoke. Cedric and his friend backed away, waving handkerchiefs in front of their noses.

'Fine boat,' said Pegleg appreciatively.

Gussie nodded. The boat had belonged to his father. She was eighteen feet long, pine planks on an oak frame, with a Lister diesel. She was good and solid. Gussie looked after her well, sanding and painting her each year. The boat was real life, as far as Gussie was concerned.

As they chugged towards the big waves to the north, Pegleg smoked his pipe, while Gussie pointed out landmarks: Cromwell's castle, King Charles' Castle, and Gun Hole where the waves built up compressed air in a narrow cave till it

38

blew back with a *boom* you could hear for miles. A gannet dived like an arrow from a hundred feet up, *ploof!* into the ink-coloured sea.

'Gosh,' said Pegleg. 'Was that an arctic skua?'

'Gannet,' said Gussie.

'Of course,' said Pegleg. 'Spray in my eye.' But Gussie thought he wasn't much of birdwatcher if he couldn't tell the difference between a gannet, which dives for fish, and a skua, which is not only a different size, shape and colour but gets its food by chasing gulls till they vomit and catching the mess in its beak.

He chugged round the outside of Men-a-Vaur, so Pegleg could see the kittiwakes. Some of the early nesters were teaching their young to fly. Male and female kittiwakes nest on rocky ledges. When the young are fledged, they are booted off into space. The little ones learn to fly quickly, before they hit the sea; they get one chance and one only.

But Pegleg didn't seem interested. He had his binoculars trained on the far horizon, where the mackerel boats bobbed, scooping up fish for delivery to the factory ship anchored off St Mary's. Gussie could see no birds in that direction, and thought he might be bored.

'You here to watch terns?' he said.

Pegleg lowered his glasses. 'Ah, yes,' he said. 'Very keen on terns.'

'They're off to the west,' said Gussie.

'We must go and have a look,' said Pegleg. 'One day. When the other chaps aren't here. Hate crowds, y'know.'

Gussie nodded. Then a thought occurred to him. 'A mate of mine said something unusual about terns,' he said. 'Roseate terns in

Shropshire. Usually they're at sea or on the coasts. Funny they should be so far inland.'

Pegleg didn't answer for a minute. When he did, his voice sounded strained. 'Who was this? Sounds interesting.'

'Dark, my mate.'

'Ah,' said Pegleg. It sounded like a long sigh. He looked at his watch. 'Eleven o'clock already,' he said. 'How time does fly. Back we go, I think.'

And back they went.

Mr Hulbert the English teacher was a brown man with a large, brown moustache. He sat behind his desk and called the roll with gloom. Gussie Smith's face was missing from the back row, where he made the bright boys sit. The fact that it was missing today was (in Hulbert's opinion) a tragedy. He knew that there were others who did not share his opinion.

One of them was waiting in the corridor after the bell rang.

'No Smith,' said Welfare Snell.

Hulbert shook his head. It was mystifying; Maurice Tanner knew Gussie better than anyone, and Gussie would rather put his finger in the light socket than let Maurice down.

'Well,' said Snell. 'He's had his chance. Mr Tanner said he'd come in today. There's only one thing for it: Plymouth tomorrow.'

'You're the Welfare Officer,' said Hulbert. 'Have you checked?'

'Oh yes. I have made quite, quite, sure.' Snell smacked his thin lips. 'He is a truant of his own free will. I must say it is very disappointing when they let one down like this. *Most* disappointing.'

'Go to hell,' said Hulbert. He turned on his heel

and walked quickly off in the direction of the staff room.

Behind Snell's heavy spectacles the little eyes glittered and shone. From his narrow chest there came a phlegmy chittering. His bony shoulders shook and his lanky hands washed each other.

Welfare Snell was laughing.

# 4

Tresco Abbey Gardens sprawl over seven acres of rocky terraces on the side of a low hill. In early days, the men of Scilly were pilots navigating tall sailing ships all over the world. When they returned from their travels, they brought with them seeds and cuttings; gums from Australia, pines from California, cactus from Mexico, palm trees from Africa; and other lesser-known plants from lesser-known places, tangling and twining.

Dark was sitting in a sort of hammock formed by the looping strands of a creeper that was found only in the rain forest on the side of a volcano in New Zealand. It did not bother Dark that it was an exceptionally rare plant. All he was interested in were the many dark-green leaves that were concealing him from his medium-good mate, James Pender, prowling the sandy paths below. James wanted his cigarettes back. Dark took a final puff of the final cigarette, stubbed it out in an amazingly rare flower, and tossed the empty packet into a nearby flowerbed.

'Dark!' shouted James Pender, seven or eight rhododendron bushes away.

Dark did his demon laugh, slid down from the creeper, and walked quietly away. Time to toy with James a little. So he passed under a

*Metrosideros* tree, whose branches had trailed new roots to the ground until the tree had twenty or thirty trunks; and he climbed into the lower branches and did a Tarzan call, banging his chest with his hands. He heard James Pender go puffing by. He did not shout again, because he wanted time to think about Gussie. It looked like Gussie had had it. Something that could have been guilt stirred in him, but Dark would not have recognized guilt if he had seen it in a glass case in St Mary's museum. In a manner of speaking it was his fault that Gussie was in trouble. But Gussie had been mad to go looking for that tape recorder with Pegleg when he knew Dark had it all the time. It wasn't Dark's fault if Gussie acted stupid like that. He felt a vague twinge of regret, which was about as sad as he was capable of feeling. In Dark's view, finders were keepers, losers weepers, and the devil take the hindmost. Life was not easy on Bryher, and you had to be hard to survive. That was what his dad said, anyway. His dad was hard; everyone knew that, including the police.

Dark began to feel unaccountably gloomy. When he felt like this, it was always a good idea to have something, well, *solid*, in his hand. Maurice should have finished the tape recorder by now. He crawled out of the fig tree, dusted off the knees of his jeans, and started across the garden in the direction of Maurice's hut.

The breeze hissed in the windbreak pines and rattled the sword-like blades of the palms. It was getting late; the sky was darkening. Once down in the garden the air was still. Dark thought it was a bit spooky; he was not quite sure why. His own breathing seemed loud, and his footsteps made too much noise on the fine grit of the path. He stopped suddenly, holding his breath. Silence. Or was it? He thought there might have been one last footfall after his own, possibly on one of the paths running parallel to the one he was on. He peered through the foliage. Nothing.

When he started to walk again he tried to move quietly, but still he thought he could hear feet keeping time with his own. The gardens lost their friendliness. Suddenly he thought of the stone heads of Neptune, the blank-eyed figureheads by Maurice's house; an eagle and a writhing serpent, the corpse of a shipwrecked man buried in the ancient abbey overrun with skinny creepers. Dark began to run.

Just ahead was Valhalla, the cloister of figureheads behind which lay Maurice's hut. The brightly-painted wooden faces grinned vacuously. Dark walked across the twilight lawn, trying not to look.

One of the figureheads moved.

It had red cheeks, black hair, and popping eyes. It was dressed in an oiled-wool guernsey and an expensive anorak, and it seemed out of breath. It said, 'Ah, the birdwatcher. Seen any roseate terns in Shropshire lately?'

Dark could feel his heart thudding and his knees trying to knock. But (he reminded himself) he was hard. 'Dunno what you're talking about,' he said.

Pegleg took a step closer. His pink face shone with sweat, and he was chewing nervously at the inside of his mouth. 'You took my tape recorder,' said Pegleg.

'Dunno . . .'

Pegleg lifted his stick and hit his artificial leg a blow that made it clang like a gong. 'TELL ME!'

he roared. He staggered, leaned against a pillar, and took a couple of deep breaths. 'Sorry,' he said. 'Bit hot and bothered. Had to run through the garden, y'see. Look here, d'you know what it's like, having only one leg?'

Dark had to confess he didn't.

'Well,' said Pegleg, sitting down heavily on a cannon. 'It's not much fun. People pity you, you see. They think you're some sort of cripple, when actually you've just had a bit of bad luck. Anyway. I haven't told anybody about falling into the sea, yesterday. I don't like to, somehow. That was why I didn't give you anything for salvaging the leg. I was, well, ashamed.'

Dark nodded. He had never talked to a one-legger before, and it was interesting. Besides, he could smell money.

Pegleg rummaged in his pocket. 'So I'd like to give you twenty pounds for the tape, er, recorder.'

*Twenty pounds.* Dark felt dizzy. His ears roared and his head spun. But he had the presence of mind to say, 'Each.'

Pegleg untrousered another twenty and rustled it between thumb and forefinger. 'Where is the tape recorder?'

Dark jerked his thumb at Maurice's hut. 'You'll keep quiet, though?'

'Mum's the word,' said Pegleg. 'Cross my heart and hope to die.'

'You don't have to do that,' said Dark, who had grown out of solemn oaths.

'Shake hands, then.'

They shook. Dark issued directions. Pegleg departed for Maurice's hut leaving Dark alone with two twenty-pound notes and his conscience.

\* \* \*

Gussie went up to Maurice's shed in the early evening. He had already said goodbye to the people in Old Grimsby, at the far end of the island. He could see that they didn't really believe he was going. But each time he said goodbye to someone, he became a little more certain. By the time he got to Maurice's shed, he was feeling very gloomy indeed. So gloomy, in fact, that he was pinning everything on Maurice somehow magically getting round Welfare Snell. Grannie Dole did not seem to have realized what was going on. Gussie did not like to think what would happen when she found out. There was an old shotgun in the attic, and it would not be beyond her to use it. GREAT SCILLY SIEGE, said the newspapers in Gussie's mind . . .

As he walked between the rows of sprouting ferns towards the shed, he expected Maurice's voice to boom from the speakers. But there was nothing. When he went in, the room was quiet and still, the computers turned off and the radio

silent. Maurice was sitting in an armchair in the corner, staring into space.

'Hello,' said Gussie.

Maurice said, 'Hello,' flatly, as if he were thinking of something else.

There was an awkward silence between them. Finally, Gussie said, 'I came to say goodbye.' He was alarmed to find himself close to tears.

'Goodbye,' said Maurice, brusquely. 'But before you take off you might tell me one thing. Why are you so eager to get off the island?'

The monstrous unfairness of it took Gussie's breath away. '*Me?*'

'And you know what they'll do to Grannie Dole, don't you?'

Gussie clung to one of Maurice's swinging-rails for support. 'I don't . . . I don't know what you mean,' he said.

Maurice's voice became coldly angry, as if he were delivering a commentary on a particularly sloppily-made radio he was mending. 'Yesterday you came to me with a letter from Snell in your pocket. A final warning. You got me to ring Hulbert and square things for you on condition that you went to school this morning. And did you go to school? Did you hell! You were mucking about in your boat. So now you've let me down, and made Hulbert look silly, and I don't know what they'll do with Grannie Dole. Gussie, I think you're nuts.'

'But . . .' said Gussie.

'And what's more I have never, ever known you to tell a lie. And here you are fibbing like a tinker, to everybody you meet. What the hell is going on?'

'*I have not been telling lies,*' said Gussie. The

47

whole terrible day seemed to be crumbling about him, and his life with it. 'If you will listen, I'll tell you.' Maurice looked surprised, and fell silent. 'I saw Snell after I left you last night. He showed me a bit of paper that said I had to go to Plymouth on Wednesday. Tomorrow. So I didn't go to school today because I was saying goodbye to a few people . . .'

'And chugging about in your old boat. You were seen.'

'Look,' said Gussie. 'He showed me a letter that said they're chucking me off the island tomorrow. I'll never be allowed a boat at Uncle Guy's. So it's not very surprising I want a last go, is it? Besides, Grannie Dole needs the money.'

There was a silence. Finally Maurice said, 'Snell gave you a letter?'

'Saying I had to go on Wednesday. Official.'

'Last night, this was. And today he was telling Hulbert that he hadn't seen you. That because you hadn't taken advantage of your last chance he'd have to have you shipped off. But all the time he *knew* he'd served you notice the night before and that was why you hadn't turned up. Snell. That twisty little herring-gutted creep!' He paused. Finally he said, 'Sorry, Gussie. Make us some coffee, could you? Extra rum in mine because we've got some thinking to do.'

As Gussie boiled the kettle his hands shook with hope. Maurice always thought of something. But this evening, Maurice wasn't on form. 'Trouble is,' he said, breathing rum fumes, 'Snell got the council to write that letter, and it'll take a council meeting to unwrite it. Put a tape on, could you? Anything you like.'

Gussie went to the rack and pulled down a case

48

with Abba written on it. He and Dark liked Abba at the moment. He fed the tape into the deck and turned on the amplifier.

'. . . note the custard yellow head and neck in the mature adult,' said the tape. 'The female gannet makes her nest with thousands of others on tall sea-girt rocks . . .' Gussie switched it off. 'That's not Abba,' he said. 'Reminds me of somebody else.'

'Your friend Pegleg,' said Maurice. 'It's that bloody Dark again. Pinching my tapes, now; he must have switched that one for Abba. Sometimes I wonder about young Dark. I really wonder. I'll have something to say to him next time I see him.'

'I'll take it down to the quay and get someone to deliver it,' said Gussie, slipping the cassette into his pocket.

'Yes. But right now what you'd better do is trot off home and get that letter Snell left you, and come back up here so we can have a look. Whatever happens, we'll fix Snell.' He smiled at Gussie, his thin face full of hollows, the light gleaming on teeth and earrings. 'Hop it, then. See you.'

Gussie trotted out into the gathering dark. There was a stiff breeze, once he had left the garden. He ran under the whispering gum trees on the Abbey Road, hearing the snipe drumming beside the Great Pool. Old Maurice could save him from Snell if anyone could.

High above New Grimsby there is a cairn of granite boulders shaggy with grey-green lichen. Between the two topmost boulders there stood a man, smartly dressed in a grey suit. He lowered the binoculars he had been using, replaced his spectacles, and started down the hill. The heather tore at the skinny white legs above his nylon socks, leaving red weals. By the time he arrived at the house on the fringes of the huddle of cottages below, he was in a terrible mood. But behind the spectacles the pebbly eyes glittered, and his thin lips were drawn back from his big teeth in a huge, ghastly grin. He took the door knob of the house in his hand. Then there was another voice: Gussie's. He turned the handle and pushed.

'Good *evening* to you,' said Welfare Snell. Gussie was holding a paper in his hand. Snell recognized it as his Care Order, strode across the room and twitched it away. 'Where are you going with that?' he said.

Gussie did not answer. He glared at Snell with hot eyes.

'Surly little brute,' said Snell. 'Going to Maurice Tanner, were you? He can't help you, you know. It's off to Plymouth with you. They're good with little savages in Plymouth.'

'I'll go where I like,' said Gussie.

Snell walked quickly across the room and grabbed him by the ear. 'Where is your room?' he said. When Gussie didn't answer, he said, 'It's your room now or St Mary's tonight. Which?'

'Room,' said Gussie.

'Bleedin' Nartzy,' said Grannie Dole, beginning to recover from her dumb amazement.

'They don't like that language in the Bide-a-Wee Home,' said Snell, with a mocking snigger. 'Now, Smith, cooperate.'

And two minutes later Gussie was in his room, listening to the key turning in the lock and Snell's footsteps receding down the stairs.

# 5

Sir Horatio Bastable was a Permanent Under-Secretary, owner of the yacht *Good Impression*, and president of the Civil Service Birdwatchers' Club. A lot of civil servants who did not like birdwatching joined in order to suck up to Sir Horatio. It was all right when they were watching Canada geese in St James' Park. But when they all had to go on *Good Impression* for what Sir Horatio called the Annual Treat, they hated it. Thanks to the mighty Atlantic Ocean, the Civil Service Birdwatchers' Club had not eaten anything but pills and dry toast for a week.

Sir Horatio Bastable liked to think that he was one of the Old School. That was why, below decks, the *Good Impression* looked a bit like the inside of a cigar box. The companionway off which the cabins of the Civil Service Bird-watchers' Club opened was made of dark maho-gany. Inside each of the cabins were two bunks, a chronometer ('in case,' Sir Horatio said, 'any of the chaps wants to do some celestial naviga-tion,') and a washbasin. Normally, Civil Service Birdwatchers quite liked the washbasins, which were useful for being sick into. They did not like the two bunks, because it is pretty undignified to have to share a room with anyone if you are a civil servant. And they ignored the chronometers. Once, a particularly keen Third Secretary had done a bit of navigating in the hope that Sir Horatio would be impressed. Unfortunately, the position he had worked out turned out to be a number eleven bus shelter in Battersea, and Sir Horatio had called him a silly twit. This incident had become a well-known part of history, and nobody had tried since.

A ghastly evening in the saloon had just ended. It had been one of Sir Horatio's famous Ludo Bees, and the civil servants were deeply fed-up – none more so than Cedric Entwistle and Philip Winstanley, who were lying, one above the other, in their bunks, staring furiously at the ceiling and hating Pegleg Hopcraft in the next-door cabin. The reason they were hating Hopcraft was that he had got a cabin to himself because Sir Horatio thought he might be embarrassed about his leg. It was jolly unfair.

Through the thin partition they could hear him bumping around. There was a groan of springs as he sat heavily on his bunk. Cedric Entwistle thought he could hear him breathing. Philip Winstanley waited for the creak of his leg-straps. Suddenly, rock music blared through the wall.

'TURN IT DOWN!' roared the two civil servants as one civil servant. The music stopped, instantly. They cleared their throats in embarrassment and simultaneously began to snore. In the next cabin, all was silent.

In the next cabin, Pegleg Hopcraft sat on his bunk staring at the cassette tape in his left hand. His normally rosy face was grey with horror, and his teeth tore at the nails of his right hand.

52

'Oh,' he was saying in a tiny voice. 'Oh gosh. Oh gosh. What will I *do*?'

Gussie could hear Snell's voice droning away in the kitchen, but he could not make out individual words. Snell would be telling Grannie Dole exactly why it was a good thing that he was separating her from Gussie ... Gussie ground his teeth with rage and sat down on the bed. On the walls, his posters shone. He would be able to get more posters in Plymouth. Plymouth was full of shops, and he could get a paper-round to earn some money. His room at Uncle Guy's would be comfortable, overlooking the back garden of the house opposite ...

'*Ugh*,' said Gussie. He knew it was no good saying it was unfair. People like Snell just *were* unfair, and it was no use complaining. You might as well complain about death or accidents. Still, if he could just talk to Maurice again, and Mr Hulbert, perhaps something could be worked out – not for his own sake, but for Grannie Dole's. But it was too late, he would be on the chopper in the morning, and that was that. The only thing left was to pack. He began to pull the bag from under his bed. Then he kicked it back. Rather than go to his Uncle Guy's he'd sleep in a hollow log. Even the bait shed ...

*The bait shed.*

Gussie's hair stood on end. Of course! All he had to do was miss the chopper! If he could spend the night in the bait shed and get to his boat first thing, he could hide behind a rock until the chopper had taken off, then get over to old Hulbert and see if he could untwist what Snell had twisted up. He was a fair bloke, old Hulbert.

Gussie leaped to his feet and tried the door.

The door, of course, was locked.

He went to the window.

Outside the window was a thirty-foot sheer drop on to granite boulders.

Gussie lost control. He kicked the door – twice – and shouted some things at Snell that stopped Snell talking for a bit. Then, when Gussie had stopped kicking and was beginning to feel ashamed of himself, Snell sniggered. It was not a Welfare Officer's snigger, but the snigger of a nasty little man who had managed to bully two people he didn't like. Suddenly Gussie understood an awful lot about Snell. But understanding didn't help.

Slowly he turned to the wall and began to take down the posters. Below, the voices fell silent.

Half-an-hour later, something clattered outside in the darkness. He went to the window. It was pitch black after the light of the room. Something whizzed past his nose and crashed against the wall. From below him came the sound of continuous, old-fashioned swearing. The voice was Grannie Dole's.

As his eyes became accustomed to the gloom, Gussie saw her far below, at the foot of a ladder from Arthur Pender's shed. The wind was up, and Grannie was wrestling. Gussie caught the top of it, propped it against the wall, and almost slid down it. Grannie Dole was panting. The ladder was a terrible weight for her. 'Get along,' she said. 'Get along.'

'Welfare?' said Gussie.

'Put one er me sleeping pills in 'is tea,' said Grannie Dole. 'But 'e fell off 'is chair on to the pocket with yer room key in it and I couldn't

move 'im, nasty Narzy. So I got the ladder.'

'Thanks,' said Gussie, feeling the beginnings of an uncertainty.

'Now you get along and summon 'elp,' said Grannie Dole. 'Keep out of the way but summon 'elp,' said Grannie Dole. 'Because I ent going to that Bide-a-Wee.' Her hard old claw of a hand squeezed his. 'I'm countin' on yer, Gussie,' she said, with her witch's grin. Then she went back into the house.

Gussie trotted off in the direction of the bait shed. As he ran through the buffeting wind, the uncertainty grew. It was one thing to appeal to Maurice and Hulbert about the dirty deeds of Welfare Snell; it was another to drug Snell and flee. Gussie admitted to himself with a nasty, sinking sensation that drugging welfare officers was undoubtedly one hundred per cent against the law, and hard to explain away.

Summoning 'elp was going to be a problem.

Gussie was extremely tired by the time he

reached the bait shed. He let himself in, lay down on a pile of old sacks in the corner, and shut his eyes. Tired as he was, he could not sleep. This was partly because the day's events marched past in grisly sequence; it was also because, besides him and the sacks, the bait shed's only occupant was a huge barrel of dead mackerel and rock salt, mixed. The mackerel and salt were topped up whenever anyone had any of either spare, which was quite often. This meant that the stuff at the bottom of the barrel had probably been there three years and could now leap tall buildings at a single bound.

At last Gussie dozed off. In his sleep he was dimly aware that the night-sound of the waves was growing louder, the rattling of the shed door more urgent. Because he was used to listening for such things, he knew the wind was freshening.

But for the moment he slept, a thin, fair-haired boy in a ragged grey jersey, with a thin face and big, dark circles under his eyes.

He awoke at first light. The smell was appalling, and he turned over to bury his nose in the sacks. As he turned, something dug into him. He reached down with his hand and felt in his jeans pocket. It was the cassette tape he had taken from Maurice's. Pegleg's tape; the one he was going to give back.

Outside the window, the sky was greying with the dawn. Halyards clattered loudly against the masts of anchored boats. When Gussie put his head cautiously round the door, the wind flattened the hair against his head. Force six; the sky was clear, studded with the final stars. The wind would get bigger.

At least Snell wouldn't be out looking for him.

Snell didn't like boats, or wind. It was time to drop the tape back on the yacht so old Pegleg would be off his conscience too.

Cedric Entwistle and Philip Winstanley had had a truly awful night. First there had been Pegleg's burst of rock music after the tribulations of the Ludo Bee. Then something seemed to have got into old Pegleg. First he had started banging and crashing around in his cabin, and woken them up so they had had the trouble of going and waking up the cook to make them some instant coffee. And then he had stuck his head round the door, and seen them in the corridor, and said a word that was not at all civil service before slamming the door rudely in their faces. Cedric and Philip now sat on chairs at the after-rail, sipping coffee and hating the wind and Pegleg in about equal quantities. Cedric was speaking of his skin, which came out in purple blotches if he got up too early, when Philip raised a hand to silence him. From astern chugged an ancient motorboat. At the tiller there stood that gangling, hungry-looking boy who had taken Pegleg joy-riding the previous day.

'What can he want?' said Cedric, who did not like being interrupted while discussing his blotches.

The boy was holding up a black cassette tape. 'Could you pass this to Mr Hopcraft?' he said.

Philip said, 'Oh. Most irregular.'

Cedric was about to point out that he was not a messenger boy when he had an inspiration. Pegleg was in a terrible rage. Why not enrage him more by sending this, well, this peasant down to him . . . 'I seem to remember him saying he'd give a reward for it,' he said.

Philip's face went blank with admiration. 'Yes,'

he said, catching on fast. 'Down the companionway, third door on the left. Can't miss it.'

The boy did not look enthusiastic about the possibility of a reward, but he tied up his boat, climbed on to the deck, and went down the companionway. Philip and Cedric rubbed their hands with glee, waiting for the explosion. None came. Still, it was the thought that counted.

'More coffee, I think,' said Cedric. 'I believe I can remember how to make it; I watched Cook most closely.'

Philip shook his head. 'Cedric,' he said, 'you are probably the most practical person I know.' Giggling, they went below to the galley.

'What do you want?' asked Pegleg. His face looked strangely sunken, as if someone had let half the air out of him.

'Maurice said you had the wrong tape,' said Gussie. 'I brought you the right one.' He held it out. Pegleg gazed at it for a moment as if he could not believe his eyes. His hand came up, and he took it, still staring at it. A slow tide of pink edged up his face; Gussie could see him swell. It was uncanny, and slightly horrible. 'Thank you,' said Pegleg, in a hoarse, trembling whisper. 'You have no idea . . . Thank you. Come in.'

Gussie mumbled an excuse. He wanted to be on his way before the dawn was properly up. But Pegleg grabbed him by the arm and pulled him into the cabin. 'I insist,' he said. 'Boys like Coca-Cola, don't they? Look, got one here.' He rummaged in a small fridge. The cabin was very tidy, Gussie noticed; as if Pegleg had packed up ready to go somewhere. To complete this impression, there was a large, black suitcase on the bed.

Pegleg thrust a can into his hand, and whipped a little silver flask from his pocket. 'Cheers!' he said. 'If you were a bit older I'd offer you a snort, hah!' His eyes were bulging from his head again, his face a deep, dangerous red. 'Bit early in the morning, 'course.' A thought seemed to strike him. 'Hello! What are you doing here so early in the morning?'

'I was out in me boat,' mumbled Gussie. He had no desire to explain. The light in the porthole was growing. 'Had the tape. Thought I'd drop it in.'

Pegleg's nose was beginning to twitch. 'And your clothes look as if you've slept in them, and you stink of rotten fish.' He sat down. His glistening face seemed to soften, and he said, 'Look here, old man, don't you think you'd better tell me what's going on?'

The only person who ever called Gussie 'old man' was Maurice. It came as a shock to hear it from Pegleg. It made Gussie want to trust him, though he knew it was crazy. But it was as if he were a kettle with the lid nailed down. If he did not let out what he had bottled up inside him, he was going to explode. But tell Pegleg? A stranger? He clamped his teeth tight, and put down the can of Coke. 'I'm in a hurry,' he said, with the last of his strength. 'I'd better be going.'

'Got to get to school, I suppose,' said Pegleg, 'in case that chap Snell comes after you again.' He picked up a handful of books and shoved them into his suitcase, resuming the packing Gussie had interrupted.

'No,' said Gussie.

Pegleg carried on packing. 'What, then?' Gussie could tell he wasn't really interested, but the kettle inside him was boiling over, and he had to tell someone.

'They suspended me,' he said. 'They're sending me away this morning.'

This did catch Pegleg's attention. He stopped packing. For some reason Gussie could not fathom he laughed and said, 'You're leaving this morning? Well, well, now!'

Gussie did not like being laughed at. 'They think I'm going. But I'm not. I'm taking off in my boat so I can get time to explain, later,' he said.

Pegleg sat down. 'What is it that happened?' he asked.

Gussie told him. When he had finished, Pegleg stared out of the porthole at the white horses chasing each other down-channel under the big wind. 'I suppose,' he said at last, 'that it's all my fault, in a sort of way.'

'Not really. It just happened,' said Gussie. He was beginning to regret telling Pegleg, who was after all on the wrong side. Maybe he had told Snell where to get off; but he was, after all a grown-up, and grown-ups were usually hostile to the idea of missing school, no matter how good the reason.

'Sorry,' said Pegleg. Gussie had the curious feeling he was being talked to as an equal – as if Pegleg thought of him as part of some conspiracy he himself did not yet know about.

'I'd better be off,' said Gussie.

'Big wind,' said Pegleg.

'I can manage.'

'Sure you can,' said Pegleg hastily. 'Thing is . . . could you take me with you?'

'What for?'

'Fancied a boat trip,' said Pegleg. 'Thought . . .
well, I'd like to go to St Mary's. I wonder if you
could drop me off?' He was on the edge of his
bunk, staring at Gussie with his goggle eyes as if
he were trying to hypnotize him. Gussie didn't
like it much.

'Sorry,' he said uneasily. 'I'm going round the
north. I can't take the chance of being spotted
before the chopper goes.'

'That'd be fine. Fine. Then you could drop me
on St Mary's after.' Something was going very
wrong, but Gussie couldn't work out what.
'Look, I've got you into trouble, and I'd really
like to put it straight. *Please* take me to
St Mary's.' Pegleg was pleading now.

'Can't,' said Gussie firmly. 'Boat leaves the
quay at nine. It's seven now. You can catch that.'
That, he reflected, was the boat he would be on if
they were loading him aboard the chopper.

Pegleg sighed. His podgy hand rummaged in
the suitcase for a moment. 'I feel awful about
this,' he said. 'But I'm afraid . . . well, please do
exactly what I tell you.'

Gussie's eyes travelled down from Pegleg's
face to Pegleg's right hand, which had emerged
from the suitcase and was now resting on his
knee. In it was something that looked like a toy,
chrome-plated and tiny, with a hole in one end
and a handle at the other. But Gussie knew from
the new expression of deadly seriousness on
Pegleg's face that it was not a toy.

It was a gun, and a real one.

'Now listen to me,' said Pegleg.

# 6

Gussie blinked, hard. The cabin was as it had
been, heavy wood panelling, the top bunk empty,
the bottom one bearing Pegleg and his suitcase.
Beyond the porthole, the spray was flying.
Everything, in short, was as usual, if anything
could be described as usual on a morning like this.
Except the gun. And the gun, somehow, seemed
silly. Members of the Civil Service Birdwatchers'
Club did not (he told himself) go around pointing
guns at boys who were just about to perform
desperate deeds like deliberately missing the
chopper so they could negotiate with their
school.

But the gun kept pointing at him, and Pegleg's
eyes bulged in their sockets with a dreadful
vitality. For the ten seconds that it took Gussie
to realize that he was in a new and extra-
dangerous kind of trouble, the world stood still.
As the silence was becoming unbearable, Pegleg
spoke again.

'You will go out of the cabin and on to the
deck,' he said. 'You will walk slowly and carefully, because I will be pointing this gun at the
back of your knee and if I have any trouble I will
shoot you there and you will never again walk on
two legs. You will carry my bag for me, and we

will move very, very quietly. Do not feel tempted to shout for help.' He tapped his tin leg. It rang softly, like a muffled bell. 'It is no fun hopping through life on one leg, I can assure you.'

Gussie nodded. Something had happened to his throat. It seemed unlikely that he could have spoken his own name, let alone shouted for help.

'Let's go,' said Pegleg.

As they went down the passage, Gussie began to think a little more clearly. Why was Pegleg so anxious to get to St Mary's? What difference did it make if he went now or by the boat from Tresco quay at nine o'clock? Shopping? At this hour of the morning the shops weren't open. Anyway, no one would threaten to blow a leg off just because he wanted to buy a few postcards. As they came to the foot of the companionway leading up to the saloon, Gussie decided that Pegleg probably didn't want to go to St Mary's at all. He began to feel very slightly relieved.

'Up,' said Pegleg. The relief evaporated. He began to climb. As his eyes came level with the floor of the saloon, he heard the sound of somebody yawning. He froze. The person who had yawned was the owner of the feet filling the blue canvas deck-shoes a yard from his eyes. Very slowly Gussie bent his knees and crouched. The deck-shoes began walking. The door on to the deck slammed with a crash. Below him, Pegleg was swearing quietly.

'Urrh,' he was saying. 'That was old Ghastly Bastable. We're running late. Wait a bit. He'll go forward to do his exercises.' It would have felt nice and normal if it had not been for the gun sticking into Gussie's knee. 'I'll get into your boat first. I'll take a tarpaulin and get under it.

Then you come, and cast off. And I'll be watching you.'

Gussie swallowed. 'Do you really want to go to St Mary's?'

The gun twitched violently. 'Mind your own dashed business,' said Pegleg in a tight voice. 'Do as you're told.'

Gussie crept into the saloon. He kept low, raising his head only to peer rapidly at the deck. Ghastly Bastable had gone forward. He was facing over the bows, swinging Indian clubs in a dangerous manner. The back of his neck was bright red.

Pegleg came up the companionway. He sidled towards the door like a great crab, his pop-eyes fixed on Gussie over the snout of the gun. Then he opened the door quietly and said, 'Where's your boat?' Gussie pointed. Pegleg lay down and wriggled backwards on his belly, puffing, the gun never leaving Gussie. He was obviously finding it difficult to wriggle, pant, and keep the gun trained all at the same time. Now was the moment. Gussie tensed. All he had to do was slam and bolt the saloon door, leaving Pegleg on the outside, and start shouting for help.

But if he started shouting, he was finished. Pegleg would be foiled, true. But Gussie would be a marked man. Snell would get his hands on him, and he would be on that chopper before he could say 'Welfare Officer'. And all Pegleg had to do was drop his gun overboard and call Gussie a burglar . . .

No. The only answer was to keep quiet, and to see about Pegleg and the gun later.

'*Oof,*' said Ghastly Bastable from his place in the bows.

'Come on,' hissed Pegleg, levering himself down the side on his belly. Gussie's hair prickled. Suddenly and for the first time, it occurred to him that it might be better to be in Plymouth with Uncle Guy than . . . dead. But by that time he was dropping into the boat and Pegleg was backing under the tarpaulin forward of the engine cover. And it was too late. Besides, he wasn't sure he wouldn't rather be dead than on the mainland.

He pushed off. The white side of the yacht receded beyond a strip of clear water.

'Where do you want to go?' he said.

'North,' said the muffled voice from under the tarpaulin.

Gussie swung the handle of the engine. The single cylinder caught with a cloud of black smoke and a heavy chug. The wind howled at him as he turned the boat's nose into the seas, and pillars of spray leaped skywards from Shipman's Head.

It looked like a bad blow.

As Dark opened the garden gate of Grannie Dole's cottage, he was feeling very slightly pleased with himself. It was an unusual feeling for him; at least, the feeling was not unusual, but its causes were. Dark was about to perform a public-spirited act.

It had started after school the previous night. Hulbert had come looking for him after class. Dark was not keen on being looked for by masters, because he knew they were seldom out to shake his hand and tell him what excellent essays he was writing. But Hulbert had cut him off at the pass.

'Seen your friend Gussie Smith?' said Hulbert, fiddling with his moustache in the way Dark thought so stupid.

Dark shook his head. 'Got to go, sir,' he said.

'Well, if you see Smith you might tell him . . .'

'In a hurry,' said Dark. ''Scuse me, sir.'

'I'm not,' said Hulbert. 'If you see Gussie, you tell him to get up to see Maurice Tanner. Mr Snell's after him, too, but I'm going to have another talk with him tonight.' He looked really worried.

Dark felt a bit shocked. Hulbert was only a master. It wasn't as if he was human or anything. So why was he putting on this act? 'All right,' he said. 'But I won't see him because I'm not going off the island.'

Hulbert looked at him too hard for comfort. 'Aren't you?' he said. 'That would be unusual, eh, Dark?' Dark felt his feet beginning to shuffle uncontrollably. They always did when he was losing a battle. 'Perhaps you're not too keen to see

Gussie now. The tape recorder, and so on?'

Dark's fingers clenched convulsively on the bank-notes in his pocket. The crackle they made was practically deafening. He was amazed that Hulbert did not seem to hear it.

'Where did you get that tape recorder, Dark?'

They were standing in Star Lane, a steep granite-paved street rising towards the castle that dominates St Mary's Quay. Hulbert moved to one side and leaned against the wall of a house, hands in the pockets of his corduroy trousers, shrewd eyes fixed on Dark's. Dark couldn't stand it. Before Hulbert could move he had sprinted past him and away through the town and to the maze of caves at Issacampucca. He did not come out until it was quite dark, and then he made his way by roundabout means to Mrs Pender's, where he lodged.

He should have been feeling pleased with himself. But curiously enough as he lay in bed he kept thinking about Judas Iscariot and thirty pieces of silver, or in his case, forty quid. After all, Gussie was supposed to be his mate. Dark did not set much store by mates. But the laws of salvage were something else. Nobody would think he was being soft if he took Gussie's share of the money over to Gussie. In fact, it was the hard thing to do. Dark began to feel better.

He got up at six, hitched a lift with the mail boat, and had himself transported across to Carn Near. Snidger the boatman told him to be sure and catch the nine o'clock back, because it was looking dirty. There was a nasty short chop in the channel, and it had rained in the night. Windborne sand hissed in blizzards among the dunes on the south end of the island.

'*First the rain and then the wind*

*Your topsail halliards you must mind,'*
muttered Dark as he trudged down the Abbey
Road. But he should be able to catch the nine
o'clock boat easily. See Gussie, and off. Do his
public-spirited act; after all, fair was fair.

Very pleased with himself indeed, Dark
knocked hard on Grannie Dole's peeling door.

When nobody answered, he went in.

Grannie Dole was in her chair by the table. She
seemed to be asleep. Of Gussie there was no sign.
Dark cleared his throat loudly a couple of times.
Grannie Dole did not move. Her ancient chin was
sunk on her nasty black dress, and her mouth was
open. A strand of grey hair had escaped from
under her peculiar black hat; it hung in front of
her face, and fluttered every time she breathed.
Her breathing had a strange, snoring quality.
Dark felt an awful dread. He lifted up her hand
and let it fall again, limply, with a thump. His
knees began to turn to jelly and he clung to the
kitchen table, staring at the large gap where her
false teeth were coming away from her top jaw.
She must have had a turn, he realized. Heart
attack, or stroke, or something.

Most people at this point would have gone for a
doctor. This would not have been like Dark, for
whom doctors represented Authority. He wanted
advice, or failing that, to spread the blame a bit.

'Gussie,' he called. 'Gussie!'

He rushed round the house. It was empty. No
Gussie. And his eye roved out of the window
across to the harbour, where the angry wind was
tearing the tops from the waves and hurling them
far inland as clouds of spray. Gussie's boat was
not there.

Returning to the kitchen, Dark sat down with

his back to the ghastly form of Grannie Dole and wondered what on earth he did next. If he caught the nine o'clock boat back to St Mary's, and got the doctor then, it might be too late. If he went to Maurice Tanner, Maurice would start asking what he was doing island-hopping at this hour, and because of his deal with Pegleg and the twenty quid he was not particularly anxious to be asked. He decided that what he had to do was find a telephone and dial 999. Maybe Gussie had already gone for help, and that was why his boat wasn't there. Dark sat and frowned. Suddenly he jumped convulsively. His eyes opened until the whites showed all the way round the irises, and his skin lifted in thousands of goose pimples.

It sounded like the crunching of very rusty gears, combined with a leakage of air from an old set of bellows half full of mud. It was coming from Grannie Dole's chair. It was the most horrible sound Dark had ever heard. Grannie Dole, or whatever spirit had crept into her ancient frame, was laughing.

'Hur, hur, hur,' chortled Grannie Dole. 'Give you a turn, did I?'

Dark smiled weakly.

'Make us a cup of tea. Git on with it,' said Grannie Dole. 'I thought you was that Snell when you come in and I didn't know you wasn't till I got a peep at yer. Give you a right turn, hur, hur, hur.'

Dark slammed the kettle on. He felt angry after his fright. 'Where's Gussie?' he said.

A look of extreme cunning crossed the old woman's gipsy-like features. 'That'd be telling,' she said. 'They's coming to take him away and he wunt be took. Not Gussie.' A blast of wind raked at the roof-tiles; somewhere nearby, a chimney pot fell with a tinkle of smashed earthenware. 'So he's gone where nobody unt find him. Kettle's boilin'.'

Dark made the tea. He wasn't quite sure what to do.

'Nasty old day,' he said.

'I bin listenin' to the wind,' said Grannie. 'Yellin' and screamin'. Take more than a wind to get young Gussie, though. He'll be hidin' up in the ferns nice and snug.'

'His boat's gone,' said Dark.

Grannie Dole's cup crashed into its saucer. 'Never 'as,' she hissed. There was a frantic note in her voice. 'Never would. He's a good boy, our Gussie. He never would take out a boat in a wind like this. He'd be bloody mad. When his mum and dad drownded on the Crim it wasn't even a wind like this en. He never would.'

'He has,' said Dark.

There was a knock on the door, and in came Welfare Snell. His pebbly eyes swept the room, checking, and his bony hands writhed round each other.

'Good morning,' he said. His eyes rested clammily on Dark. 'Come to say goodbye to your friend, Smith, have you? Hurry up or you'll be late for schoo . . .'

'He's gone,' said Grannie Dole, the horror in her voice temporarily yielding to a vast satisfaction. 'Clean gone where you won't find him, you nosey varmint.'

Snell smarmed his shiny hair with his hand; he seemed not to understand. 'But I left instructions for him to be kept in his room . . .'

'And I letted him out,' said Grannie Dole with

glee. 'Who you think you are, you horrible little greasy, tellin' folks what to do in their own homes?'

Dark watched with great pleasure as Snell's pale complexion turned paler still. But Snell said nothing. Instead, he turned to Dark. 'Where has he gone?' he said.

Dark shrugged. 'I heard you were putting him on the chopper,' he said. 'Maybe he's come over early to St Mary's to be sure he catches his flight.'

Grannie Dole laughed shrilly from behind a cloud of kettle steam.

'Very funny,' said Snell. 'He'll catch his flight, though.'

'Nasty rough day,' said Dark. 'Could be too much for the choppers.'

Snell's eyes narrowed with rage behind his glasses. In his view, the islanders used weather as an excuse far too often. What was a bit of wind beside the might of the Ministry of Education?

'Smith didn't think there was too much for his boat, I see,' he said. 'It's not at the moorings.'

Grannie Dole stopped giggling abruptly. 'Boat gone?' she said, remembering. 'Oh.'

'Skulking behind a rock somewhere, no doubt,' said Snell contemptuously. 'Silly child . . .'

'Just you bleddy well hold your tongue,' said Grannie Dole in a voice of surprising firmness. 'If that boy's out in this blow, he's in a turble fix and no mistake. I doan want him back on a plank like . . . they others.'

Dark knew she was talking about Gussie's parents, and he swallowed to fill the hollow that had opened in him. 'What shall we do?' he said.

'Go and find him,' said Welfare Snell.

'Lifeboat's out,' said Dark. 'I heard the maroons 'safternoon. Ship in trouble fifty mile to the south, shifting containers.'

'So that's that,' said Grannie. 'You run up to Maurice and you tell him what's what, and we'll see.'

'Will it get thick, Grannie?' said Dark.

Grannie Dole looked out of the window with her ancient, rheumy eyes. The sky was clear as a bell. The rocks with their mantles of spray stood high above the horizon, as if they were closer than they really were.

'Look at the loom of Hangman's Island,' she said. 'Yur, e'll thicken.'

Welfare Snell could not believe that he had stood listening to a senile woman and a truant brat telling old wives' tales while one of his charges was absconding from a Care Order. He snorted and strode out, slamming the door. Dark followed at the run, bent on his own errand.

Grannie Dole remained alone, crumpled in her chair by the table. High in the rafters, Mr Wilson the cat stared at her in amazement. For Grannie looked suddenly shrunken, and her hand was clawed and shaking. From her black clothes there rose a new smell, different from the fustiness of not too many baths. Mr Wilson knew it from mice he had caught and played with.

It was the smell of fear.

Outside, Dark caught up with Snell. The wind had risen even while they were in the house. It was becoming difficult to stand without leaning into the gale at an angle. Snell was watching the spray hissing inland from Plumb Island, and his tongue came out and moistened his thin lips.

Dark watched. A demon entered him. He said, as quietly as possible over the howl of the wind, 'Mister Snell, I do believe you are skeered.'

Snell darted a glance at him that rolled crazily behind his spectacles. He laughed a false laugh, and fell silent. Suddenly his face looked naked and vulnerable, and Dark could see that Snell was just a futile little man who wanted to be respected – or if not respected, feared. In Dark's view, that was his problem. He ran off towards Maurice's hut, propelled by the gale at his back.

# 7

'North it is,' said Gussie.

*Good Impression* slid astern, and the boat's nose moved steadily down the long rock-sided gulley of the harbour. Even here, where there was some shelter, the seas were so big that it was like driving over a roller-coaster. On the starboard bow, Gun Hole boomed like a cannon as waves rushed into its cavernous mouth. Ahead, Shipman's Head and the Kettle Rock smashed the waves to shreds that hung across the mouth of the harbour in a curtain of spray so fine it was almost like fog. It was a horrible day to be off the north: a deadly day. Gussie braced a leg either side of the bottomboards, slitted his eyes against the wind, and concentrated on keeping his boat head to sea. Round his ears the storm howled.

He had almost forgotten about the man who held him at gunpoint until Pegleg crept out from under the tarpaulin. And all was not well with Pegleg. He seemed to have lost interest in the gun, because he wedged it between the thwart and the engine and sat down heavily. He was a nasty greenish colour, particularly around the nostrils. After a couple of minutes' silent thought, he stuck his head over the side and was very, very sick. The sight gave Gussie a good deal of satisfaction.

They were passing out of the harbour now, and the waves were immense. The boat humped up a long, long hill, steepening towards the top. Fifty yards to starboard, the black teeth of the Kettle punctured the slope in a horrible suck of white foam. The wave steepened and curled. Gussie watched its overhang, feeling the heavy chug of the engine driving him up and into it. White water roared down the port side and the bottom-boards dropped away like a descending lift. A colossal explosion sounded to starboard as the crest hit the Kettle and water fountained a hundred and fifty feet into the air. Then they were ploughing down the long slope on the far side.

The waves seemed in some curious fashion to steady Pegleg. Though his face was a dreadful colour, the green tinge had left the area round his nostrils and he picked up his gun again.

'Where do you want to go now?' Gussie yelled above the roar of the wind.

'Round the top of the island,' said Pegleg. 'Down the other side.'

Gussie nudged the tiller with his thigh. The boat began to crawl to starboard, meeting the waves with its port bow instead of head on. Pegleg stared at them, crest marching on crest, awe-struck. The wind plastered his hair to his bullet head. 'Is it dangerous?' he asked. Then for some reason he bent double and began to laugh, a cracked hysterical laugh the wind tore to rags.

Gussie did not answer. It was not only dangerous; it was as near suicide as made no difference. Nobody in his right mind would be out in weather like this. The saw-toothed horizon was empty. Even the mackerel boats were in shelter, having

75

delivered their catches to the factory ship anchored off St Mary's.

Pegleg's laughter died away. He edged astern, the gun cradled loosely in his hand, the spray running down his face. There was something different about him, Gussie thought. He looked younger, as if some tightly-wound spring inside him had run down. He started to talk again, but Gussie was not listening and, in any case, could not hear properly. He was in a sort of dream, exhausted but very clear. What he had to do was keep hurdling these waves, one after the other, until he had rounded Round Island. Then he could turn down inside Black Rock and weave his way down until he was at the back of Tean. On Tean he could hole up until the chopper had gone. And from there he could go and find Hulbert. He would have two days' grace, then; the weather would see to that. Gussie had read the signs, and he knew what was going to happen next.

Already a smudge of grey was showing on the western horizon, and the wind was backing. One depression was following hard on the heels of the last. What they were in for now was rain, and fog as well, and still with winds of force eight and up. With visibility down to fifty yards, nobody was going to be flying choppers. It was good weather to stay hidden in.

But what was he going to do about Pegleg?

'Where are you going?' Pegleg demanded.

'Back of an island,' said Gussie. 'Hide.'

They were coming round Round Island now. A hundred yards to starboard, the spray was roaring up to mix with the white towers of the lighthouse, three hundred feet above the sea.

'Not that one,' said Pegleg. He looked frightened.

'No.' Gussie was silent a moment, turning the boat in the smooth bottom of a trough, with the next wave hanging twenty feet over him. The sky wheeled. The stern rose, and the crest passed under. To the southward, the low brown hulk of Tean came clear of Round Island. Its shores were spattered with white foam, but nothing like the roaring horror on the north of Tresco.

'Are we going to be all right?' said Pegleg nervously.

It seemed a rather odd question, coming from a man with a gun in his hand. 'Long as the engine keeps going,' said Gussie. Then, 'Why are you pointing the gun at me?'

'Why do you think?' said Pegleg. 'To make you do what I want.'

'But I was going to do it anyway,' said Gussie. 'Come round the north, I mean, and hide out.'

'Oh,' said Pegleg. He looked suddenly awkward and twiddled the gun round his finger in an embarrassed manner. His fat cheeks went pink. 'So it wasn't, um, necessary. I see.' Clearing his throat in a preoccupied manner, he shoved the gun back in his pocket. But Gussie noticed that he kept his hand there.

Gussie said, 'So I suppose I've got to take you to St Mary's, then?'

For some reason Pegleg looked even more embarrassed. His eyes strayed from Gussie's to the crest of the next wave. Gussie prayed briefly. A couple of bucketfuls of foam sloshed into the boat, but the engine gave them just enough forward way not to ship any more. 'Are we safe?' asked Pegleg again.

'As long as the engine keeps going and you

77

keep bailing,' said Gussie. 'There's a bucket under the tarpaulin somewhere.'

Pegleg started bailing as two more waves rolled under. It was all very well being able to see the calm water; but it was taking a long time to get there.

Pegleg now seemed to be thinking. He had put the bucket aside and had the gun out again. He pointed it at Gussie and made beckoning movements with his free hand. Gussie stooped into the lee of the engine cover. Out of the wind, it was possible to talk almost normally.

'Ghastly thing,' said Pegleg, over the thud of the diesel, 'but I'm afraid I've got to drop you overboard.'

Gussie hoped he hadn't heard right. 'Overboard?' he repeated.

Pegleg nodded and shrugged his shoulders. 'Awfully sorry,' he said. 'But it can't be helped.'

'Oh,' said Gussie. Somehow the world seemed to have gone completely batty. It was hard enough to believe that Snell was trying to ship him off to his Uncle Guy's, and that he had taken to the high seas in a force nine gale. It was even more peculiar to be hijacked by the irritable but not really dangerous Pegleg. To hear Pegleg threatening to put him into the sea was, well, bizarre. And now he came to think of it . . .

'Well I suppose I do owe you an explanation,' said Pegleg. He had backed away into the bows, and the gun was rock-steady. 'What can you see behind me?'

Pegleg's eyes were cold and hard. Gussie found that he was horribly frightened. He searched the waste of foam and jagged rocks ahead. The mackerel boats were anchored a couple of miles down there, against the loom of St Mary's. Otherwise there was nothing unusual. 'Fishing boats,' said Gussie, with a dry throat.

'And a factory ship,' said Pegleg. 'Yes?'

'Yes,' said Gussie.

'And where does that factory ship come from?'

It was like a geography lesson in Hell. 'Dunno,' bawled Gussie down the wind.

Pegleg's cheeks were shining again, big and fat and full of blood. 'Company called Fishco,' said Pegleg. 'Some of them are friends of mine. And when you've gone over the side I'm going to take your boat and chug on down and get aboard that Fishco ship.'

'Why?' said Gussie. He was inching his foot towards the engine, tiny bit by tiny bit. 'What's so special about Fishco?'

Pegleg grinned at him, a grin of great complacency. 'Not much,' said Pegleg. 'But fishing boats can pick up a lot of information, and my friends at Fishco pass it on to . . . certain governments. I've worked for them for some time, now. Made myself useful by sending a few messages when they wanted them – some trade figures here, a couple of sheets of statistics there. You know how it is.'

'Yes,' said Gussie. 'You're a spy.'

Pegleg burst out laughing, his pop-eyes creasing with mirth.

'How over-simple,' he said, shaking his head and failing to notice Gussie's foot, which was continuing on its way towards the engine casing. 'Spies! I was only helping the spread of information, and now of course I am going back to . . . the certain country I've been working for to claim my pension. I regret very much that I must drop you

79

overboard. I shall do it near an island so with any luck you won't drown. Nobody will find you until the factory ship is long gone; meanwhile your boat will have been discovered holed, and all will assume you drowned while running away from your Snell.' He giggled. Gussie's foot found the knob on the deckboards, and gave it a sharp shove. It was the fuel cut-off.

The boat's nose went down as her stern lifted to another wave. The chug of the engine faltered, then stopped. She slowed down, still rising on the wave.

'Cor, blimey,' said Gussie. 'Blowed if she hasn't stopped!'

The smile on Pegleg's face curdled and vanished. The silence was suddenly intense, until he realized that it was not silence, but the roar of many sounds piled on top of each other. There was the shriek of the wind in his ear, and the suck of water at the boat's bow, and the knock of the oars as Gussie began yanking them from under the seat and, worst of all, the hiss of the foam at the crest of the next wave.

Gussie, yanking at a stuck oar, looked back at that crest, and he knew he had chosen the wrong wave to cut the engine on. This one was approaching at a leisurely pace. Twenty feet above, the light struck clean through the curling green at its top. The wind died, blocked by the wall of water. Up and up went the stern in the ghastly hush.

But this time the boat was not moving forwards, away from the white water above. And without the engine and the oars, there was no steerage way, so the boat was going to take the wave not stern-on but awkwardly sideways . . .

The boards kicked under Gussie's feet as he
realized what was going to happen. He had time
to yell, 'Look out!' and then the crest had curled
over and water was hammering into the bottom-
boards and Pegleg's open mouth and on to
Gussie's head.

He felt the boat go over and he with it, rolling
and tumbling down the long slope of water and
into the stifling dark. Something had smashed
into his right shoulder and knowing it must be
the boat he grabbed it with both hands, clamping
with his left, as his right went numb. Over and
over and over they went. Gussie thought ludi-
crous thoughts; first that this was what it was
like to die; and then, this was what it must be like
to be stuck in a washing machine. He knew he
would not be able to hold his breath much longer,
but he did not panic. Instead he hung grimly on
to the boat, because a little voice inside his head
was saying, *the boat'll float, she's got buoyancy,
and if she does, you will*. But his eyes were full of
red roaring. Any minute now he was going to

have to breathe the green salt sea; and the old boat that had done in 'is mum and dad would have done him in, too. He was floating off in a haze . . .

His head broke water and he gulped air. A wave was rolling under him. He choked and looked about him. He had been on the receiving end of a miracle.

High above, the sugar-white towers of Round Island reeled against the scud. All around, the waves were huge, except where the boat lay wallowing, full of water. Here, some freak eddy in wind and current had left a calm patch – or at any rate, a patch where the waves were ten feet instead of twenty, and did not break. Gussie waited for a minute, gasping air. With aching arms he heaved himself very cautiously over the stern and into the flooded boat.

Then he remembered Pegleg.

Ten feet to starboard, bubbles erupted in the water. Gussie felt around in the flooded boat till he found the boat-hook, twitched it from its clips, and hooked violently at whatever it was that was making the bubbles. At the second attempt he met resistance, a solid weight on the end. He felt sick for a moment; what if he had hooked an eye socket or poked deep into an ear? But then he pushed the idea firmly aside and hauled in. The mass on the end of the boat-hook turned into a man, caught by the armpit of his jersey: Pegleg. A Pegleg blue-white of face, open-mouthed, with his eyes rolled up so only the whites showed. Gussie got him over the stern and from there levered him on board. Water poured from the slack mouth, and the boat wallowed alarmingly. Pegleg or no Pegleg, Gussie realized, the first thing he had to do was get some of the water out. What amazed him, suddenly, was that he felt bad about the idea of Pegleg dying. The man had after all intended to drop him overboard. Why shouldn't Gussie do the same?

It certainly seemed the sensible thing to do. After all he was a spy. But spy or no spy, Gussie couldn't do it. Anyway, Pegleg was breathing now, so it was too late.

Gussie found the bucket lashed to the thwart, and began to bail. Five minutes later, he heard feeble splashings and turned to see Pegleg bailing too.

'We'll be all right,' Gussie said.

Pegleg didn't react.

It took half an hour of back-breaking labour before she was emptied. Gussie was afraid that someone in the lighthouse would spot them; but they were still tucked into the eddy under the rock, out of view except to someone in the glass lantern. Nobody with any sense, Gussie reflected, was going to be in the lantern on a day like this.

He pulled the oars from under the thwart. By an astounding bit of luck they had not shaken free. Then he sat down, told Pegleg to do the same, and began to row. Pegleg's gun was at the bottom of the sea, a hundred feet below. Pegleg was white and flabby and looked like a spent force.

'We'll put into St Helen's,' said Gussie. 'We'll tie up at the back of the island and sit among the rocks, nice and snug.' Pegleg made no reply. 'Nobody will see us. And you can think about things for the day.' He went back into the oars and braced himself for the surge out of shelter and into the wind. It was only then that he became aware that something was different. The wind had dropped.

'The wind's gone,' said Pegleg, wonderingly. He used a normal speaking voice, but Gussie could hear him perfectly. Gussie nodded, and redoubled his pulling. Without the wind the waves were higher and longer, the beginnings of a ground sea, the huge swells that result when the sea gets its head and rolls away unabated by the gale.

'Isn't that fantastic?' said Pegleg. 'I must say I think you did well. I suppose in a manner of speaking you saved my life. And there was I about to, well . . .'

'Drop me overboard,' said Gussie between clenched teeth.

'Oh, well,' said Pegleg. 'That was only, well, a joke. Ha ha!' It was a terribly unconvincing laugh and Pegleg must have realized it too, because he unzipped his case (which had stayed jammed under the seat while the boat was capsized) and began wringing the water out of large pairs of floral underpants.

Gussie wondered if he had another gun in there. Well, even if he had it wouldn't do him much good. Unless he was much mistaken there was worse than guns on the way. He cast a nervous glance at the sky.

Something peculiar was happening up there. Until now it had been an attractive picture-postcard blue. But during the past five minutes, long, yellowish tendrils of cloud had crept in from the west, outriders for a solid wall of black that was gliding with ferocious speed across the whaleback of St Mary's, trailing a curtain of rain.

In Gussie's mind it was as clear as a weather-map on the back of a newspaper. Bad weather is caused by depressions. The wind goes round the centre of a depression like water in a vortex down a bath plug. The vortex is always anti-clockwise in the northern hemisphere. The northerly gale had been produced by a depression somewhere over the middle of England. That one had moved away; hence the calm. But now another was following hot on its heels, and the first part of it to hit would be the bottom right-hand corner, with winds from the south-west. The strength of the winds depended on the depth of the depression. This one, Gussie thought, looked as deep as a dungeon. In addition, St Helen's bay lay a quarter of a mile away, due south-west. It looked as if there were headwinds in store.

He was right. The headwinds came.

They ripped along the troughs, tearing a new swell from the flanks of the old. The boat corkscrewed viciously and the oars bucked and slammed at Gussie's chest. Over the islands poured the wind, pasting the hair against his neck and flicking at the oar-blades as if they were feathers. He fought it. After a while Pegleg said, 'We're not moving.' He sounded frightened again, and his jowls quivered with cold.

Gussie was working too hard to reply. Directly behind lay the open sea. Behind and to starboard across a mile of waves and rain and wind-torn spray, lay the lump of White Island. White Island was lonely: White Island was uninhabited and seldom visited. White Island was a brilliant hiding place. And best of all, White Island was downwind.

Gussie pulled hard with his right oar. The

islands turned about him. A last gleam of sun lanced the rugged cliffs of cloud, pinning the boat like a moth. Then the world vanished under a hissing mantle of rain. Gussie pulled with his right until he felt the wind on his right cheek. Then he began to row.

It was all rain now. All he could do was to keep the wake more or less straight and hope for the best. The boat moved at dizzying speed, the wind chewing at its counter. He heard Pegleg shout and then they were between two rocks on the foreslope of a swell, water hissing from under the boat's belly as she surfed. Well inside the Lion Rock, thought Gussie; on course. To the north the waves were banging like dynamite. Then Pegleg shouted again, and as Gussie looked over the side on top of a wave he saw that underneath there was not water but large, round boulders. The wave went from under and the boat crashed down with the sound of splintering wood and did not come up again. Gussie opened his mouth to shout, but it filled with water, and he could feel the planking of his dear boat disintegrating. He heard Pegleg again; then a bigger wave got him and twitched him off the seat and flung him end over end. And for the second time that day he thought, so this is what it feels like to die.

# 8

After he left Grannie Dole's house, Snell trotted off across the island, poking his nose here and there. He was half-convinced that Gussie was still on the island. So he went through a couple of pinewoods, and trod in a pheasant's nest, and got himself sworn at by the game-keeper who was practising his bagpipes where he thought nobody could hear him. After that he went rummaging through the rubbish dump in the quarry at the top of the island and put his foot through a bicycle wheel and couldn't get it off. While he was hopping about tugging at the wheel he tripped on some old fence wire and fell into a plastic bag of something very nasty that must have come from the hotel kitchen at about Christmas time, by the smell of it. The Snell that emerged from the dump was a white-lipped and raging Snell with a bad ankle, torn trousers and a right shoe full of nameless filth. And the rage was entirely directed at Gussie Smith. He stood on top of the bank that hid the dump from view. At his feet the sea stretched away to the north, splattered with foam. Although the wind had dropped, he was pleased to notice, the waves were still angrily big. He hoped the weather was going to take a turn for the better. He did not look behind him and see the clouds racing up from the south-west. This was partly because (as the men on the islands frequently said, frequently in his hearing) Snell knew as much about Scilly as a pig knows about football. There was another reason, too.

Rage had sharpened Snell's eyes until they were keen as an eagle's. What he now saw made them bulge until they practically rattled against his spectacles. Far away, in the rosette of white water surrounding the steep-sided sugar-loaf of Round Island, he could see a tiny speck. With the sixth sense that had made him one of the most remorseless and hated welfare officers in England, he knew that this was his quarry. From his pocket he whipped the miniature binoculars presented to him by his relieved colleagues at Pinner East, the day he announced he was being promoted away from the Pinner area. In the circle of their magnification he saw the boat wallowing in the swell and Gussie, hair plastered to his head with water, bailing with a bucket. There was someone else in the boat too, but Snell did not bother to find out who. Nor did he ask himself why Gussie might be tipping water out of the boat with a bucket, or whether he might be in trouble. His mind filled with words like *culprit, miscreant,* and *the long arm of the law,* Snell hurried down the hill towards New Grimsby harbour.

As he walked, clouds rolled across the face of the sun. He paused to train his binoculars on the boat under Round Island now heading for White Island. Snell noted Gussie's course, and his thin lips twitched in satisfaction as a swathe of rain hissed across the water hiding his quarry from view. He was pretty sure he knew Gussie's plan.

New Grimsby harbour is a long beach of white sand, facing north-east and backed by grey, granite houses that are backed in their turn by the heights of Castle Down. One of its great virtues is that it is beautifully sheltered from the south-westerly gales that for centuries have been the scourge of mariners round Scilly. Welfare Snell, scuttling along the concrete road in the direction of the hotel dinghies tied up above the high water mark, was feeling the beginnings of fear. He could feel no wind, of course; that was consoling. (It did not occur to him that where he was walking he might be sheltered). Still, it was rather a long way to White Island in a rowing boat.

By the boats, a man Snell recognized as Mr Pender was smoking a cigarette. Seized with a brilliant idea, Snell hailed him. 'I say,' he said. 'I'd like you to row me over to White Island.'

Short Henry Pender was an experienced seaman. He knew that the only people out in boats today were the loony, the desperate, or the just plain ignorant. He also disliked Welfare Snell. So he did not answer immediately, but blew smoke in the rain and stared at Snell in what Snell could only regard as a deeply offensive manner. Finally he said, 'Row your horrible self,' and stumped off in the direction of the public bar at the New Inn, which would be opening in five minutes.

Short Henry did not for a moment expect that Snell might take him at his word. Short Henry might be a lot of things, but he was not a murderer.

Snell watched his retreating back in baffled rage. His hatred of these ... *disorderly* little islands had been stirred up by Dark's taunts. Now it boiled up and overflowed. He laid hands

89

on one of the dinghies and tugged. It slid down the beach and into the water. He would show that Smith child who was boss. He'd catch up with him if it killed him.

Oars and rowlocks were already in the boat. Snell settled the oars and began to row with the windmill strokes he had learned on the pond at East Pinner Park. The shore fell astern at satisfying speed. So did the shelter of the houses and Castle Down. Snell felt the first puff of wind on his face and stirred nervously on his seat. With the next puff, he began to think better of the pursuit, and started to try to turn round. In the process he somehow lost one of his oars overboard and before he could pick it up the wind, now blowing unhampered by the land, had caught the dinghy. The land receded at terrifying speed.

'Help!' shouted Welfare Snell. 'Heeeeeeelp!'

But nobody heard. The yellow and blue dinghy surged remorselessly downwind until it was hidden by the veils of rain. Out of the grey rain came the heavy explosions of wave on rock.

Maurice Tanner hung up the mike of his VHF set and pulled himself up on a set of steel bars. 'Nothing,' he said to Dark. 'Nobody's seen him.'

'Maybe he's in the bracken,' said Dark without much conviction.

'Maybe.'

'Er hum,' said a voice on the VHF. Even distorted by passage through the ether, it sounded plummy. 'Calling all, er um, stations.'

'Clown,' said Maurice. 'Doesn't know his radio discipline.'

'We were wondering if anyone had seen one of

our chaps. Oh, yes, sorry, this is yacht *Good Impression* calling, yacht *Good Impression*, moving down to channel 24.'

Maurice lowered himself into his chair and clicked the big dial on his transmitter receiver until the green LCD on the panel said 24. 'Come in, yacht *Good Impression*,' said Maurice.

'Oh hello,' said the plummy voice. 'Sir Horace Bastable here. We think a chap of ours, name of Hopcraft, went off in a boat a couple – no – sorry, three hours ago and my captain says that if he's out in a boat in this weather he's in trouble.'

'Is he alone?' said Maurice.

'We presume he started off, as I say, three hours ago with a young boy who had been taking him birdwatching lately and well, honestly, we're all a bit worried here.'

'Any idea where they were going?' said Maurice in a thin, tight voice.

'I saw them heading north.'

'And you didn't stop them?'

'Why should I have? Not my business. And look here, my good man, I do not like your tone of voice . . .'

Maurice waited with his teeth clenched while Bastable explained exactly why he did not like his tone of voice. Finally he said, 'And you've seen no sign of them since?'

There was silence, filled with the atmospherics of the gale.

'No.'

Maurice twisted savagely at the dial until the LCD shone 16, the number of the emergency channel. 'All stations,' he said. 'All stations. Missing last seen heading north up New Grimsby

91

harbour. Gussie Smith and passenger Hopcraft, in open fishing boat SC2454, repeat SC2454. Please report sightings, channel 24.' He tuned down to Channel 24. The dim, greenlit shed filled with the wash of static. There were no human voices.

'Make me some coffee,' he said at last to Dark. 'Extra rum.'

Dark did as he was told, properly frightened now. He could see Maurice's thin face deeply shadowed in the corpse-coloured light, gold earrings glinting as he muttered into the VHF mike. As morning turned into afternoon, Maurice's shoulders slumped further and further. There was no news of Gussie.

Short Henry Pender came rollicking back down the hill from the New Inn. He had had a jolly time in the pub, and was looking forward to a nice afternoon in the shed out of the rain and wind, painting up the last of the hotel boats for the summer season. Actually Short Henry was planning a quick kip on a pile of sacks in the corner, but he was a conscientious worker so he was not admitting this, even to himself.

Trudging along the beach road with his shoulders hunched round his ears to keep the rain out, he came to a sudden halt. Either he had had a lot too much rum up there in the New Inn, or . . .

He counted the boats again. There had been six. Now there were five. Short Henry was no mathematician, but he knew what this meant. One of them had gone. Marching down the beach, he did exactly what Sherlock Holmes would have done: he examined the sand at the edge of the water. And sure enough, there were foot-prints and the mark of a keel.

Short Henry paused for a moment, swaying slightly as the meaning of the tracks sank in. His rather bloodshot eyes scanned the howling murk to seaward. 'Strewth!' he muttered. Then a certain line of reasoning began to form in his mind, and he grinned.

He walked the hundred yards to the hotel, lighting a fag as he went. The manager took a look at his boots and tried to keep him out, but Short Henry pushed him aside with a lordly jab of the elbow. Entering the telephone cubicle, he dialled 999 and asked for Police. A police voice on St Mary's asked if it could help him.

'Yes,' said Henry Pender with great satisfaction. 'I'd like to report that Welfare Officer Snell from the pesky Council has pinched one of my boats. Watcher going to do about it?'

In the last two hours, Maurice Tanner had aged by ten years. Dark was getting more and more frightened. Maurice was usually so full of force that it was somehow obscene to see him slack and despairing in his chair. Normally no one noticed that his legs didn't work; but now, the whole of his body seemed to take on something of the awkwardness of the way that they lay under his desk. The computer screen cast green lights over his hands, straying across the strings of a little Irish harp from his musical instrument case. He was playing dismal runs in a weird minor key. Dark was powerfully reminded of horror videos. He shifted uneasily in his chair, thinking he couldn't stand much more of this.

The telephone rang. Maurice put the harp down and picked up the receiver. It was Hulbert, from St Mary's School.

'Any news of Smith?' said Hulbert.

'No,' said Maurice heavily.

'We've had the police on,' said Hulbert. 'Apparently Snell's pinched one of Short Henry Pender's boats.'

'Has he?' said Maurice. 'I hope they lock him up.'

'Quite,' said Hulbert. 'But the interesting thing is that I think he was probably chasing Smith.'

'He went round the North,' said Maurice. 'In a big sea . . .'

'But suppose he got round,' said Hulbert. 'Just suppose that he wanted to hide somewhere while the chopper went, and that he decided nobody would be looking to the north on a day like this . . .'

'But he had that one-legged bloke with him,' said Maurice. 'Hopcraft.'

'I know,' said Hulbert. 'That's the only bit that doesn't make sense. But just ignore him for the moment. There he is, round the North. Where would he go?'

'Could be anywhere.'

'I suppose so. But I reckon he would have got round there after breakfast time, and that was about the time Dark said he saw Snell go looking for Smith. I can't imagine Snell going boating for the fun of it. My bet is that he must have seen Smith and gone after him.'

'So where is he now?'

There was a silence on the line as they both thought about where he might be now. Neither of them liked the conclusions they reached.

'So,' said Maurice at last. 'Snell pinched a boat from Short Henry. Short Henry's painting up the hotel boats. He keeps them at Old Grimsby. Snell wouldn't have set off while the wind was onshore at Old Grimsby; he wouldn't have been able to make any headway. So he must have gone off either when the wind dropped . . .'

'No,' said Dark. 'He wouldn't have had time.'

'Or after it had gone round to the south-west. Does he know anything about boats?'

'He knows water's wet.'

'So. He's probably halfway to Wales by now. Or on White Island, if he's lucky.'

'White Island?'

Maurice sighed. A tiny glow of hope had begun to warm him. Perhaps Snell had gone to White Island deliberately, because he had seen Gussie there. 'I suppose,' he said, hope cooling, 'we'd better have a look. I'll get Short Henry, and we'll be off.'

'What about this Hopcraft bloke?'

'Dunno,' said Maurice. 'Probably birdwatching.' But he knew that was not an adequate explanation. And he knew that although Hopcraft might have been birdwatching this morning, by now he was probably dead.

Dark pushed Maurice down the island in his wheelchair. They went fast with the wind behind them; on the steep hill above New Grimsby, it was so strong that the chair would have sailed up unaided if Dark had let it. But he did not. He was numb now; earlier he had wriggled, trying to convince himself that none of this was his fault. But it *was* his fault; if he hadn't pinched the tape recorder none of this would have happened. For the first time in his life Dark was feeling the pangs of guilt. Their unfamiliarity made them extra painful.

A crowd had already gathered on Old Grimsby
quay, huddled under umbrellas and oilskins in
the driving rain, drawn by the strange bush tele-
graph that links islanders in times of disaster. At
the front of the crowd, in the centre, stood
Grannie Dole. She was wearing a black straw
bonnet transfixed with many pins. Someone was
holding an umbrella over her but she was already
wet, and the black dye from the hat was running
down her face in streaks. When she saw Dark she
reached out and grabbed him by the arms.

'You can stay 'ere with me, my man,' she said.
'Bear I company.'

'Aren't you going, Grannie?' said Maurice.

'No I ent,' said Grannie. 'I'll know soon enough
and I've seed too many on ... planks. I hates
planks.'

Dark stood beside her without protesting. She
was still as marble. Suddenly he felt a violent
pain and looked down. Mr Wilson, the cat, was
half-way out from her long black skirt, and had

sunk his teeth into his ankle.

'Ow,' said Dark quietly. He did not want to make a noise because he knew this was all his fault and he knew that Mr Wilson knew, and he did not want anyone else getting ideas. Dark was pretty overwrought. He waggled his ankle furtively. 'Stop yore wriggling you eel creature,' said Grannie Dole. 'Stand quiet.'

So Dark stood quiet. And the boat, with its men and blankets and hot drinks, chugged heavily into the thick rain and fog, and vanished.

'We'll be near now,' said Short Henry to Maurice. 'You can hear Lion Rock breaking.'

The fog was thick around them, the sea steep and murderous. Short Henry did not look worried, but he was. Maurice was confused by the roarings and boomings about him; he was used to the small, delicate noises of his shed. He kept hearing things borne on sudden gusts: voices shouting, seagulls crying. Now he heard a diesel engine thudding, just for a second. He told Short Henry, and Short Henry said politely, 'Oh, ah.' Maurice could tell that Short Henry didn't believe him. Come to that he didn't believe himself.

Short Henry could have found the entrance to the White Island lagoon blindfolded and with his ears stopped. In the calm lagoon, he cut his engine back and motored slowly, peering into the twenty-foot circle of vision that was all the fog allowed. It brushed Maurice's face with the fingers of a ghost, and he shivered. Something bumped against the bottom, and Short Henry moved the boat into reverse. They looked overboard, at the thing that had bumped. It was long

97

and waterlogged, dark as a whale. Once it had been a boat. Gussie's boat.

'Maybe they're ashore,' said Short Henry, unhappily.

An hour later, he was back. Maurice looked at his face and did not have to ask what he had found. Silently, Short Henry started his engine and shoved the throttle on to the stops, and they began the long, sad hammer through the mad seas back to Old Grimsby quay.

## 9

An ant was marching through the short grass. It paused to twiddle its feelers immediately under Gussie's left eye, and proceeded in the direction of his nose. Gussie was lying face-down on the turf, high above the rocky beach, his head resting on a clump of sea-pink. He watched the ant, thinking vaguely that he had better move before it wandered up his nostril. But he felt too tired.

His back and legs and arms ached as if he had been beaten with a club. And he was freezing cold – so cold that he could not control the shivers that went through him like earthquakes, starting at his toes and ending at his head. He was also extremely hungry.

There was a bright side, though. If he was hungry, cold and aching, it seemed unlikely that he was dead. Also, it seemed unlikely that he was dying. He had read enough of Dark's westerns to know that while dying people usually asked for water, they seldom requested steak and chips. He lay for a moment contemplating the vision of Lee van Cleef sprawled under the desert sun, his parched lips framing the syllables, 'Porridge, porridge!' Then, without thinking about it, he got up.

It was not a good idea. The sea, or what he

could see of it in the grey rain, spun around him, and he dropped to his hands and knees. It was at this moment that he remembered that he had forgotten Pegleg. And with the memory of Pegleg came a kind of half-picture of himself swimming with agonizing slowness across the lagoon; of shallow water, then rocks with seaweed and clots of oil and driftwood; and after that lichen and, further up, grass ... And that was as far as the memories went. He was quite happy to leave them at that because they weren't particularly pleasant.

What, though, had happened to Pegleg?

He lifted his head again. He was in a hollow above the beach of boulders that edged the lagoon. That accounted for the fact that he was in the shelter; the wind was howling over him and not through him. The wind itself blew as strongly as ever. The sky was grey and ragged and low as the roof of a cave. Out in the channel it came down and touched the heaving black water. It was as dirty a day as Gussie remembered. The lagoon was calmer. Gussie searched it anxiously with his eyes, feeling something like hope. Far out towards the bar of round boulders something as long as a whale wallowed low in the water. The hope flared up like a firework and died. It was his boat, all right. But it was a boat in name alone. The waves rippled sides as limp as paper, smashed to a pulp. At the waterline, chips of painted wood bobbed in the waves. She was finished.

Gussie felt a tightening in his throat. It was only bad luck, he knew that. But somehow he couldn't manage to be reasonable about it. The boat had been the biggest thing in his life; it had kept him independent, his own boss. And now, just because stupid Pegleg had wanted to do things that couldn't be done and pointed a gun at him to make him do it, she was a smashed-up wreck.

For the first time, the events of the past couple of days began to rearrange themselves. It was all very well hiding out to miss the chopper. In fact he had probably missed the chopper already. But Pegleg was a spy, and Pegleg ought to be stopped. Gussie was a bit hazy about what sort of spying he had done, but it didn't really matter.

At this point Gussie's mind stopped being woolly at the edges and clicked into focus. It must be about noon. Pretty soon it would be low tide. At low tide the bar between White Island and St Martin's would dry out. St Martin's was inhabited. All Gussie would have to do was stroll across to Lower Town and make a telephone call. He began to feel less cold and hungry. It occurred to him that Pegleg was probably dead, drowned. He could not help feeling a twinge of sympathy for the man, boat or no boat, spy or not . . .

But this was no time to be feeling sorry for anyone. Groaning with pain, Gussie slid on his belly to the edge of the beach, where the foreshore was eroded into a three-foot cliff. Bending double, he began to pick his way along the beach, invisible to anyone walking on the heights of the island. As he went he thought he heard a strange scraping noise from inland, but he was breathing so hard that he couldn't be sure.

After a hundred yards the low cliff on his left disappeared, giving way to a smooth slope of heather and sprouting bracken. Gussie dropped to his belly and began to wriggle forward. Again he thought he heard the creaking, but he didn't want to look round in case the whiteness of his face gave him away. He crept on, eyes fixed always on the next-boulder-but-one ahead.

Suddenly the boulder spat at him. He winced back as granite chips whined about him and ploughed into his forehead. When he opened his eyes again there was a splash of bright metal in the groove on the surface of the stone. He could not think how it had got there until a voice called, 'Come here!' He wiped away the liquid that was trickling into his eyes. He thought it was sweat; but when he looked at his hand, he saw it was blood. He didn't care. A deadly despair was stealing over him. For up on the hill, among the big lumps of granite scattered down the side, sat Pegleg. And in Pegleg's hands there was a peculiar-looking gun with a telescopic sight.

It was sheltered here. He could hear quite clearly as Pegleg said, 'I'm sorry. Didn't mean to hurt you. But I couldn't let you off the island. I'm sure you'll understand.' Pegleg sounded as reasonable as ever.

All the aches came back. 'All right,' said Gussie. 'I'm coming up.'

'Come slowly,' said Pegleg. 'Keep in the open.'

As Gussie went, he thought quickly. Pegleg clearly did not want to kill him, or he would have done so already. It was therefore just a matter of biding his time. Meanwhile, it was vaguely possible that Pegleg had some food, and he, Gussie, was starving. Nobody seemed to get hungry in books. He made a mental note to tell Dark, when he saw him – *if* he saw him.

Pegleg was chewing. When Gussie was perhaps fifteen feet away Pegleg said, 'Sit down, old boy,' and tossed Gussie a lump of brown bread and a bar of chocolate. Gussie ate them in a silence that lasted about fifteen seconds. Pegleg stuffed a chicken wing into his mouth and said, 'Thought you were dead. Couldn't find you. Delighted to see you, of course.' Gussie thought that he couldn't have looked very hard, and that he was unlikely to be delighted. 'Sorry about your boat and everything. Nice shallow lagoon, though. I just walked ashore with my suitcase. Look here, I thought you did jolly well in that big sea. I mean I owe you my life and all that sort of thing.'

'No you don't,' said Gussie, swallowing the last of the bread. 'Spies don't owe me anything.'

'Well, if you put it like that . . .' Pegleg fiddled with the gun. Gussie thought he looked slightly ashamed with the rain trickling down his face. 'Oh, dear. I mean I ought to kill you, you know that, don't you? Because if I don't you'll rush off to St Martin's the moment my back's turned . . . No,' said Pegleg with determination. 'It's no good. I had the chance just then and I, well, I couldn't.'

'Chicken!' said Gussie, furious.

'Oh. Sorry,' said Pegleg and tossed him a drumstick.

'They'll get you,' said Gussie. 'You and your tape. They'll all be out looking for you.'

'Very possibly,' said Pegleg. He seemed completely unlike a spy. Gussie found it difficult to stay angry with him for long. Rather against his will he picked up the drumstick from the rainy grass and ate it. 'Except that they'll have to be awfully quick,' said Pegleg. He stirred uncomfortably in the grass. His artificial leg made a curious creaking noise, metal scraping against metal. Gussie drew in his breath and held it. He had had an idea.

Pegleg shifted again. 'Yes,' he said over the harsh creaking. 'Terribly sorry you got sucked into all this. It happens, you know. Happened to me, in a way. I mean I probably made it sound all very deliberate. It wasn't like that. There I was, quite happy in my job, pushing paper around a desk. Then my old Mum got ill, and well, I needed some extra money. So when a chap came up to me in Madame Tussauds and asked me if I wanted to earn a hundred pounds a week, what could I do? Mum was delighted, of course. It wasn't as if I was telling them anything important, either. Well, Mum died of course, but by then it was too late. And then I went to a conference a bit ago, and I told them about that. And everything got sort of out of hand. They sent me a miniature camera and everything.'

He was staring at the grass now, as if he had forgotten Gussie was there. Gussie was moving very slowly towards a large boulder on his right. 'And guns and a tape recorder. You know about them, of course. That cassette. And the guns . . . Felt ghastly about pointing them at you. It's no dashed joke being a spy, you know. Hey! Where d'you think you're going?' He brought the gun up just as Gussie vanished behind the rock. 'Look here, come out or I'll have to shoot!'

Gussie crawled on his belly behind the cover of the rock. When he ran out of cover he was uphill of Pegleg. Now he would see if he had guessed right. His mouth was dry, the food he had eaten like lead in his stomach. Crouching like a sprinter, he burst into the open, running uphill.

Pegleg fired twice, but the shots went miles wide. Gussie saw the first of the rocks coming up to meet him and took a flying leap behind it. From down the hill came the sound of tortured metal. Pegleg's leg was jammed. It stuck out of his trousers at a horrible angle as he crept up the hill like a wounded beetle. Gussie was glad he had been right, but he did not let himself think how glad, because he might have passed out. Being shot at, he had discovered, was so frightening it made him feel sick. He lay in the rocks and panted. Pegleg was coming closer. Silently, Gussie crept out on to the blind side of the hill and lay down in the shelter of a clump of gorse bushes. The wind hissed among the spines and desolate blasts of rain splattered his face. He was free, in a manner of speaking.

By now he was savagely angry with Pegleg. He had almost forgotten that he was on the run from Snell and his Uncle Guy. What infuriated him now was that his boat was smashed to toothpicks on the Bar, and all because Pegleg was a sort of pathetic little crook. These Fishco blokes must be pretty stupid to be taken in by him, thought Gussie. But then he remembered not only the way Pegleg had stitched up Snell, but how very close the bullet had been to his head as he crept along the rocky beach, and he wasn't so sure.

Well, Pegleg was finished now. All Gussie had to do was slip across to St Martin's, get help, and have him picked up. But Pegleg had said that anyone coming after him would have to be quick. Gussie didn't like the sound of that. And he didn't like the sound of the cassette tape either.

Indeed, the cassette tape was a bit of a mystery. Pegleg seemed to have become pretty over-excited about that cassette. He would have to be a very, very keen birdwatcher to be quite so devoted to it. But if he were a keen birdwatcher, why would he attach so much importance to a load of rubbish about roseate terns in Shropshire? There was definitely something funny about that tape, thought Gussie, staring at some rabbit droppings. He meant to ponder the question a bit longer. But there was no time. He dropped to his hands and knees, and glided down the hill towards the place where Pegleg had left his suitcase.

Gussie traversed the steep western slopes in dead ground. Somewhere above, Pegleg was creaking about. The boulders were thinning now. He was on the edge of the green patch where the suitcase was. Rain was running over its black leather. The wind plastered Gussie's jersey to his ribs, and he was freezing cold. For a moment he hung back. Out here in the wind, he couldn't hear the creaking of Pegleg's leg. To get the suitcase he would have to break cover. What if Pegleg was waiting in the rocks above with his rifle trained? Gussie shivered. Then he took off his jersey and scrunched it into a ball, tying it tight by the arms. Pulling a long, dead stick from a gorse bush he stuck the jersey on the end so it looked like a giant, woollen lollipop. Then he pushed it steadily out into the clearing.

It did not look at all like a head, Gussie thought gloomily. If Pegleg didn't shoot at it, it would probably be because he was waiting for the real thing. He shoved it out a bit further. Suddenly the stick twisted violently in his hand and the jersey flew off the end, and the ghost of two shots whipped away in the gale. Pegleg might not be

able to tell the difference between a jersey and a head, but he could hit either with no trouble. Gussie crouched behind his rock and shuddered for a bit. Then he began to wonder what to do next.

The suitcase was six feet away. If he crept across that six feet, he would be shot; it was as simple as that. Why not just nip back to St Martin's? Any sensible person faced with a hostile spy with a rifle would have done that. But as usual, Gussie found that he was quite unable to do the *sensible* thing. He had to do the *right* thing. And the right thing was to get that tape. For a moment he gazed gloomily at the fragment of stick in his hand. Then he knew what to do.

Creeping over to the gorse bush, he pulled out another branch and trimmed the thick end into a shallow hook. Then he returned to his vantage point beside the suitcase and stretched out the stick. The suitcase was the kind with a zip along the top and floppy leather handles. Gussie's stick caught in a handle. He twisted until it was firm, and started to pull. The suitcase began to slide. There was a shout from up the hill. Gussie realized that his hand was out of cover, and shrank away, still tugging. There were three shots and granite chips whirred around his hand. He dropped the stick and sucked blood from the cuts. Then, gritting his teeth, he groped for the stick and gave a swift, strong pull. The suitcase slid across into cover – jumping as four more bullets slammed into it. Gussie unzipped it and dumped it on the grass. Six pairs of floral underpants sailed away cheerfully on the gale, and a thin wail of rage came from higher up the slope. Then the creaking began. Gussie found the cassette and jammed it in his pocket. Quickly he sorted through the rest of the stuff. There was a tiny camera, and something that looked like a walkie-talkie. The sight of it struck a deeper chill into Gussie than the bullets. Crouching low, he ran to the beach. From here on round, it was two hundred yards to St Martin's, under cover all the way . . .

He skipped over the four-foot cliff and on to the boulders, crouching down to get his breath. Fear had given way to a crazy elation; his heart was beating hard, and he felt a strong urge to giggle. It was then that he saw the wreck.

It was a blue and yellow dinghy; or rather, it had been a blue and yellow dinghy. Now, it was some blue and yellow driftwood. Gussie frowned. It was not like Short Henry Pender to let his boats go adrift. But he had more serious matters on his mind now than Short Henry's rowing boats – things like national security. He patted the tape in his pocket, drew a deep breath and made ready. The bar across to St Martin's was seething with white water, but he could make it.

'One . . . two . . . three,' said Gussie, nerving himself. He lifted his foot to start.

Hard fingers clamped on his ear from behind. 'Not so fassst, Gussie Smith,' said the voice of Welfare Snell.

# 10

It is fair to say that Welfare Snell, at the moment he gripped Gussie by the ear, was halfway round the bend. The three-quarters of an hour in the hotel rowing boat, spinning like a top and hacked at by wind, rain and waves, had been more appalling than anything he could remember. The shore of White Island looming from the murk had seemed almost too good to be true. He had sat through the dreadful thuddings and splinterings that accompanied the demise of the hotel boat, white-faced but grinning, seized by a weird optimism. It flashed across his mind that he had died and gone to Heaven. This notion had become stronger when he had seen the grey-jerseyed form of Smith flitting pale and spidery among the rocks. His catching of Smith (or arrest, as he preferred to think of it) was so easy as to be practically supernatural, which cheered him up; for Snell, while he had always been pretty sure that he was going to go to Heaven, had nursed a secret terror that there might be a shortage of rules and regulations in the Promised Land.

He commenced his interrogation of Smith immediately. The boy would not answer. Instead he wriggled and twisted until Snell was forced to use his superior weight and sit on him. Snell remained in the seated position until Smith grew quiet. Around his black head the gale raged. But Snell knew his duty. He was going to sit on Smith, G., until help arrived. So on he sat, firm in his resolve and loonier than a taxi-load of chimpanzees.

And eventually his patience was rewarded. There was a strange creaking in the rain, and then Mr Hopcraft of the Department appeared, limping severely. Snell hailed him with joy. His memories of Mr Hopcraft may not have been happy, but surely a fellow member of the Department was in duty bound to help out another. At this point Smith heaved under him and began talking in a low, earnest voice. Snell scarcely listened. It was the usual farrago of rubbish. All about spies, this time. He smiled in a superior manner and bounced on Smith, to shut him up. Out of the rain, diesels chugged. Help was at hand. Mr Hopcraft pulled from his pocket an unusual-looking gun (it gave Snell quite a turn for a moment). He pointed it in the air and pulled the trigger. A green flare arched into the fog. The diesels changed direction. Offshore a patch of fog thickened and became a large grey launch, its paint streaked with rust. Twenty yards off the beach, it sent in a rubber dinghy on a long line. Mr Hopcraft and Snell took Gussie Smith each by one arm and led him down to the dinghy. Waves soaked them, but they were soaked already so they did not notice. When they came alongside the launch they were pulled in by large hands. Snell stood there and preened himself. Then he turned to one of the men in the launch and said, 'Inclement weather for the time of year, is it not?'

The man had a big flat face and eyes so narrow they had a foreign look. He stared at Snell as if he had no idea what he was talking about, then turned to his colleague and made a remark that Snell overheard. Snell felt a chill. For the first time, he began to doubt himself. The pebbly eyes swivelled to Gussie Smith, bluish-white on the bottom of the boat, his knees drawn up into his stomach. Something was wrong, thought Snell. If this were Heaven, why did the crew of the launch have FISHCO printed on their jerseys?

Gussie could not remember having felt more miserable. His teeth chattered, and his body shuddered so hard that he had a vague feeling that it might fall apart at the joints. He would not have cared. His mind had entirely stopped working. He could hear Pegleg's voice talking in a strange language. He seemed to be arguing. Opening his eyes a crack, Gussie saw him sitting beside a large, slab-faced man with slit eyes. The man was wearing a gaberdine raincoat and a slouch hat. He should have looked ridiculous, but he did not, because his eyes were like trapdoors over a mineshaft. When he looked at Gussie incuriously, as if Gussie were a pork chop he did not entirely fancy, Gussie felt a shudder of fear that was worse even than the cold.

Gussie felt Pegleg's hands going through his pockets. When the hands had finished their work, the tape was gone. Gussie felt so ill he did not care. Then Pegleg began shouting at the slab-faced man, and Slab Face shouted back. He seemed to be winning the argument. Gussie could not be bothered with it, fear or no fear. He rested his head on the wet steel of the boat's bottom, and went to sleep.

When he awoke, it was dark. He seemed to be in a small, hot room. Rough blankets covered him; through the bed he could hear a deep humming, like an engine. He lay for ten seconds with his eyes open. The room was moving. He was in a cabin on a ship. But what ship?

There was only one possibility. He was aboard the Fishco factory ship, anchored off the Hats. His bones ached, and he was very hungry. Otherwise (slightly to his amazement) he was all right. He sat up, and banged his head on the ceiling. Top bunk. As he lowered his head, he caught a faint whiff of fish. Yes, it was the factory ship. But what was that noise? It was a sort of snipping and munching – a very nasty noise. Gussie's groping hand found the light switch. He turned it on and looked at the bunk below. The noise was Welfare Snell, biting his nails.

'Hello,' said Gussie.

Snell jumped a foot in the air and came down whimpering. 'Smith!' he said.

'What's happening?' said Gussie.

'How would I know?' said Snell, with indignation. 'Except that through your criminal irresponsibility we have been shanghaied. I am in complete ignorance as to the situation obtaining.'

Working this out, Gussie realized that Snell was trying to say he didn't know what was going on, was badly frightened, and trying to put the blame on him.

'Well,' said Gussie, 'we're on a factory ship, and old Pegleg's a spy. He's had it fixed up for

113

months. He told me. They'll find our boats, yours and mine, and they'll think we drowned, Pegleg too. And by then we'll be goodness knows where and nobody none the wiser.'

Snell made a sound like a hamster being run over by a racing bike.

'But I must say, I thought it was pretty clever of you to get over to White Island,' said Gussie. Snell captive on a factory ship was a Snell with the sting removed, and even a Snell that needed cheering up.

'Pah,' said Snell. 'It was extraordinarily easy. The dangers of the sea are in my opinion heavily overrated.'

'Yes,' said Gussie soothingly. 'Now how are we going to get out of here, Mr Snell?' He looked around the cabin. It was a cream-painted metal box with pipes running across the ceiling. Except for the bunks, there was no furniture.

'Get out?' said Snell. 'I presume we shall be released in due course.'

'Well, maybe,' said Gussie, who had been doing some rapid thinking. 'But they won't let us go until we're outside the twelve-mile limit, because we'd draw attention to Pegleg and they could be stopped and searched, and that would be that as far as Pegleg was concerned. So they'll probably let us go outside the limit. If they let us go at all.'

'But outside the twelve-mile limit . . .' The ship heaved at its anchor and the deck tilted wildly, as if to demonstrate what was waiting beyond the limit. Snell seemed about to protest that it was all contrary to local authority bye-laws when there was a clunk of bolts and the cabin door opened. It was a large sailor, wearing a jersey with FISHCO written across the chest and carrying a tray. On the tray were two covered plates and two glasses of something that looked like water. Past him, Gussie could see a corridor painted the same cream as the cabin. The smell of fish had grown perceptibly stronger.

'It,' said the seaman, grinning. 'It, it.' He made great gnashing movements with his jaws. Snell whimpered with terror. Gussie seized a plate and wolfed down the stew it contained. It wasn't bad, and he said so to the seaman, who was standing there still grinning. Snell did not seem to be hungry. 'It, it,' said the seaman again. Then he picked up Gussie's glass of water, wagged his finger at Gussie, said, 'Tch, tch,' and drained it at a gulp.

Snell had been watching him. Gussie said, 'If you're not hungry, can I have your stew, Mr Snell?'

'I cannot see how anyone could eat at such a time as this,' said Snell. 'Take it, traitor.'

Gussie could not see that it was going to do anyone any good if he starved patriotically to death, so he wolfed it down. Snell picked up his glass of water. Having made his speech, he felt in need of refreshment for the vocal chords, so he drank it all at once.

Gussie, still sitting on the top bunk, felt a violent thud as Snell's head hit the bottom of his mattress. It looked very much as if Snell had gone mad, because he lurched into the middle of the floor, bent double, fanning his tongue, which was stuck as far out of his mouth as it could go. The rest of his face was an astonishing scarlet hue, and his eyes, horribly magnified by his spectacles, were firmly crossed as if he were trying to inspect a fly creeping up the bridge of his nose.

'Hkkkkkk,' he was saying. 'Gaaaaaaaaah.'

Extraordinary things were happening to the seaman, too. He had doubled over and appeared to be sobbing tragically. Peculiar foreign noises squeezed from his throat. Gosh, thought Gussie, they've been poisoned. He stiffened, feeling the hairs prickle at the nape of his neck. But then he realized that the seaman was not sobbing but laughing, and saying over and over, 'Not vater, wodka! Not vater, wodka!' and doubling over again. At which point Gussie, now brave with stew, took a flying leap from the top bunk, landed with both feet in the seaman's kidneys, and started to run down the passage. Somewhere behind him, he could hear Snell's voice. 'Come back!' he was shouting. 'Smith, they'll punish us! Come BACK!'

But Gussie ran on. At the end of the passage was a flight of metal stairs. Gussie climbed them cautiously, inched his head above the level of the next deck, and looked quickly about him. There was nobody there. Below, a confused sound of shouting had begun. A door slammed and large feet were slapping on metal. Gussie belted along the deck, catching a glimpse of rain-whipped sea through the portholes. He did not know where he was going: upwards seemed easier, that was all. There seemed very few people about. Another flight of stairs; then he could hear low voices ahead. He crept forward, and peered round the door from which the voices were coming. It was the bridge, a long, low chamber walled on one side with windows. There was a man at the wheel and a woman in a peaked, braided cap giving orders. Gussie remembered that foreign ships had female captains, sometimes. But he did not spend

116

long on the thought, because the feet were pounding behind him and he had to find somewhere to go. There was an open door on his right. Taking a deep breath, he slipped inside.

It was the radio cabin, and it was empty. But there was a cigarette smouldering in the ashtray and a half-empty cup of still-warm coffee. Gussie shut the door. There was no lock. He looked for a chair to wedge under the handle. But there were no chairs, except the operator's, and that was bolted to the deck. Gussie sat down in it, twisted the VHF dial to Channel 16, Emergency, and picked up the handset. It was not switched on. The set was unfamiliar. He hunted for the switch and put the set on SPEAKER by accident. Static roared across the cabin, deafening him. At last he found the HANDSET control. He took a deep breath. 'Calling all stations,' he said. 'Calling all...'

'Gussie,' said Maurice's voice from the earpiece. 'Where the hell are you?'

Gussie thought Maurice must have been very upset to break radio discipline so alarmingly. 'Going down to 24,' he said. You stayed on the emergency channel as short a time as possible, in order to leave clear ether for anyone else who might be in distress. Gussie found his fingers were slippery with sweat on the tuning knob. It was as if he had been in a nightmare and Maurice's voice had woken him up, and having woken up, the nightmare was continuing. Feet crashed in the passage. He got Channel 24, and said, 'FISHCO!'

The door crashed open and he was lifted from the chair and hurled across the room. He landed in a bookshelf, crashing to the ground in an avalanche of signals manuals.

The man with the slab face and the foreign eyes walked silently to the radio console and switched off the set. 'Get up, silly poy,' he said. 'Get up or I vill ask Forklift to twist you a little.' Forklift was a small man with huge hands and a black eye-patch. The hands flexed. They looked like crane buckets. Gussie found the idea of being twisted by them extremely frightening. 'All right,' he said, and walked meekly back to the cabin. As he trudged, he thought: They can't have heard Maurice. Maybe Maurice will work out where I am. But at the same time, there was no getting away from the fact that to locate him and Snell, Maurice would need to be a mindreader as well as a VHF radio operator.

The cabin smelt of vodka. Snell was looking even more glassy-eyed than usual, chewing his lips. 'Smith, you are a fool. A disobedient fool,' he said, sneaking a glance at Slab Face, hoping for approval.

Slab Face said, 'Yes, very stupid. Now be careful because on this ship we have a mackerel factory. If you behave you can go ashore in Baltic Sea, Sweden maybe. If you not behave then we have a machine in the factory hold which is useful. You can feel it humming through the deck, now. It is called the fishmealer. It is for fish we cannot put in tin cans, and it grinds them up very, very small so our farmers can spread them on fields in fine farmland of my country. I am sure you would not like to end up on a field in my country, Mr Snell. Or you, poy Smith.'

Snell made a sound like a sob. Gussie watched Slab Face's cheeks stretch in a grin that showed stainless-steel false teeth below eyes that did not share the joke. The humming that came through the deck seemed to have taken on a new and sinister note.

## 11

In Maurice Tanner's shed on Tresco, the hiss of static sounded like a long intake of breath. Maurice himself looked drawn and exhausted. The search of White Island had taken more out of him than he cared to admit. Dark had gone home. Now it was Grannie Dole who sat in the corner, zebra-striped with dye from her black hat, while Mr Wilson the cat prowled the mesh of aerials under the rafters. Maurice hung the microphone back on its hook, and Grannie Dole spoke for the first time.

'That,' she said, 'were Gussie.' She paused. Actually Gussie's voice had shaken her badly; she had resigned herself to the fact that he was dead. Death was one thing, but phantom voices from beyond the grave were another, and she was by no means sure she liked them.

Maurice nodded. 'There wasn't enough for me to get a trace,' he said. 'Gale's making some bad atmospherics, too. But it sounded like . . .' He did not continue, because they both knew what it sounded like: Gussie's voice, firm but a little higher than usual, observing his usual impeccable radio discipline. Then nothing. Not for the first time, Maurice cursed himself for insisting on radio discipline.

'He's got a cold,' said Grannie Dole. 'I heard him

sneeze, just before he stopped. Oh, he don't look after himself. But,' she said, returning to the issue at hand, 'where be Hopcraft, him that he calls Pegleg? And Snell, though if he be drowned all I say is he had it due him.'

'Wish I knew.' Maurice reached for the mike again. There were no leads, except Hopcraft. 'Yacht *Good Impression*,' he said tiredly. 'Come in yacht *Good Impression*.'

Grannie Dole remained in her corner. High above, Mr Wilson picked his way among the aerials. Her ancient eyes followed him as he nosed at a metal tube. As his nose touched it, it spat blue sparks. All Mr Wilson's fur stood on end and he leaped for what he must have thought was safety. But as usual Mr Wilson was wrong, and he landed on thin air. He crashed, hissing and flailing, into the aerials and stuck, laced like a fly in a web. Sighing, Grannie Dole climbed on a chair and began to untangle him. He snarled ungratefully. 'Funny,' said Grannie Dole as the cat withdrew to sulk on a high rafter, 'it didn't sound exactly like a sneeze. Not quite ATISHOO! More like *FISH*CO.'

Maurice paused in mid-sentence. 'Dole,' he said, 'you're dead right.' The voice of Sir Horatio Bastable gibbered from the handset. 'Is it possible,' said Maurice, cutting him off, 'that your Mr Hopcraft has any connections with that factory ship off the Hats?' The gibbering became indignant. Maurice said to Grannie. 'Ring up the coastguard, and ask them about the factory ship.' Grannie's arthritic finger stabbed the dial. Maurice said into his handset: 'No, no. I'm suggesting nothing of the kind. But if that ship weighs anchor in a force 10 gale I, personally, will know what to think.'

# 12

Later – Gussie was not sure how much later – Pegleg came to see him. Someone had mended his leg, and the noise of grinding metal had gone. But silence had failed to ease Pegleg. He looked pale and nervous. Whatever he might say about going home, Gussie thought he looked more like someone being kidnapped. Also he seemed embarrassed about something.

'Look here,' he said, 'I'm awfully sorry about this.'

Gussie wondered what he was expected to say. Perfectly all right, Pegleg, I'm having a frightfully jolly time?

'I didn't really mean this to happen,' said Pegleg, explaining.

'But on my boat you said you were going to drop me overboard,' said Gussie. 'Then you pointed a gun at me to get me off White Island. Then you locked us in a cabin. And now you say you didn't mean it to happen.' He could feel himself getting angry, but he knew it was fear as much as anger, so he made sure he kept the lid on.

Pegleg made chopping movements with his hands in the air. 'Yes, yes,' he said. 'Of course I had to keep you under control and actually yes, I might have dropped you overboard and felt ghastly about it afterwards, of course. Nevertheless I wanted you to be put ashore, um. But Splid doesn't think . . .'

'What don't I think?' said the harsh voice from the doorway. It was the slab-faced man. When he wanted to, he moved as silently as a huge cat. He seemed to frighten Pegleg, too. 'I think you should not be speaking with our young friend here, Hopcraft. I think perhaps you will be giving him ideas. Perhaps you have become soft through all this time in the decadent West. You must learn . . .' (the harsh voice had the ring of metal in it, now) '. . . that at home we do as we are told, Hopcraft.'

Pegleg grinned weakly. His pop-eyes were sad and worried. Gussie got the distinct impression that he was thinking better of his decision to retire.

'Now, Hopcraft, come with me,' said Splid. 'Soon we are pulling up our anchor. As you can hear, fishmealer is working still, even when we are at sea. We proceed at six knots, slow speed, for a while.'

Six knots, thought Gussie. Two hours till the edge of the twelve-mile limit. Two hours in which he could, maybe, find an unsecured boat . . .

'And in about an hour, we will show you how a mackerel factory ship works,' said Splid. 'You are missing education so it will be most useful. And for Mr Snell.' He laughed. It sounded like a tank running over dinner plates. 'Meanwhile, you will have breakfast. Eat heartily, my friends, for I do not know when you will get your next meal.' He laughed again, lids lowered over his slit eyes. Then he ushered Pegleg out of the cabin and slammed the door.

Breakfast was two mackerel, fried, with tea and vodka. Gussie ate hungrily. Below, Snell was whimpering like a kicked dog. He did not touch the tea or the mackerel. But Gussie was interested to see that when he offered Snell his vodka, Snell accepted. Snell seemed to have developed a liking for vodka.

After a while, Snell began. 'Oh, oh, oh,' he moaned. 'It's always the way. Boys like you lack a sense of responsibility. You are not to be trusted. People always suffer from your actions. I suppose it is ironical that in this case the one to suffer most is me. Because, of course, as you know I have always made it my business to try to sort out your life, Smith. Smith?'

Gussie grunted. He was lying with his hands under his head, gazing at the cream-coloured pipes crawling across the ceiling and thinking about other things. An hour was not long. Not long at all. He had to *do* something . . .

And as usual, while Gussie schemed what to do, Snell continued with his catalogue of important ideas. 'Take my own case,' said Snell. 'My parents lived in a very nice part of Surrey near Dorking. My father was in the Planning Department and my mother was an Income Tax Inspector. They lived a very regular life and I must say brought me up in great orderliness. And it is only fair to say that I justified their hopes for me, six O-levels and an A-level in Local Government. Not bad, though I say it myself. Of course they became elderly and none too well, but luckily there is a very nice Council Home near Dorking and they live there now, in separate wings of course, that is the way the facilities are arranged. But it is more convenient like that. For the staff,

I mean. It must be a burden for the staff. My father writes poetry.' Snell shuddered, checking what might have been further admissions. 'So of course, Smith, I am human just like you, and I do understand that in the case of an elderly person one has to make certain arrangements. As in your own case. Arrangements must be made and facilities provided . . .'

'Tell you what,' said Gussie. 'Can you scream?'

Snell said, 'Sorry?'

'Scream,' said Gussie. 'Like this.'

'I know what screaming is,' said Snell hastily. 'What for?'

'We need that door open,' said Gussie. 'So I can bash whoever comes on the head and we can get out of here. That's the first step.'

'But . . .' said Snell.

'Look,' said Gussie. 'In about forty-five minutes, they are probably going to feed us into the fishmeal machine. I don't fancy sitting here and waiting for that.' The ship lurched to port and plunged down in a new trough. 'Feel that? We're moving. Outside the islands. Won't be long now.'

'Outside the islands?' said Snell. 'But . . . I'm a Council employee . . .'

'Tell Slab Face,' said Gussie. 'Now, would you mind screaming? And lie in the middle of the floor and I'll try to get the guard in the back of the neck with the breakfast tray.' He was a bit doubtful about the breakfast tray. It was the sort of weapon that would have worked well in a film, but on a real Fishco guard it might well be different – like hitting a rhinoceros with a drinking straw. Snell's adam's apple was bobbing, and he was clucking like a hen.

'Scream,' said Gussie. 'Go on.'

Snell's mouth opened slightly, and he said 'Baaa,' like a small lamb.

The door opened, and Pegleg came in again. Snell put his hands over his ears and screwed his eyes shut. But Gussie did not hit Pegleg with the tray, because Pegleg already looked as if he had been hit, and with something a lot heavier. He was red and he puffed for wind, and his eyes bulged as if they had been blown up by bicycle pumps. He grabbed Gussie's head and said in a low, urgent whisper, 'Dinghy on a line from stern ramp. Follow pipes from mealer . . .'

'Come,' said the voice of Splid from the cabin doorway. 'Now we will go on our education tour.' He stuck the cardboard tube of a cigarette between his steel teeth. Two sailors came forward. One of them took Snell's arm, the other Gussie's. The hand gripping Gussie's arm was the size of a leg of lamb, and a lot harder. It seemed unnecessarily hard for a guided tour.

126

Gussie dug in his heels. The hand whipped him along as if he were a five-year-old, its owner seeming not to notice the check. They walked down the flights of steel stairs and in a direction Gussie recognized as aft. The ship was ploughing through huge waves with a ponderous corkscrew movement. The smell of fish grew stronger and stronger. Oh well, thought Gussie; they were going in the right direction for the stern ramp. But as the humming of machinery grew louder, the little mouse of fear that had been nibbling at his mind swelled until it occupied the whole foreground. In between him and the stern ramp lay the fishmealer.

At last they came to a heavy metal door, and Splid threw it open. When they went through, they were on a gallery in the side of a huge metal cavern lit with blue arc-lights. The faces of the men and women working on the floor of the cabin looked white and unhealthy. Machinery clattered and howled. The noise was appalling, and it made Gussie want to screw up his eyes and put his hands over his ears.

'Come,' shouted Splid. His voice was barely audible, and the arc-lights caught his stainless steel teeth. He waved a hand. 'This is superbly equipped modern factory ship,' he yelled. 'Over there is fish-hopper. In there go mackerel and are refrigerated. Then out they come and gutted and sorted immediately by operatives. Excellent fish are canned right there and not so excellent fish proceed to the fishmealer for grinding.'

Gussie saw Snell's lips frame the words, 'How interesting.' Splid did not seem to care if he were interested or not, but presumably Snell had decided that taking an intelligent interest in the

127

conducted tour might prolong his life. He was asking a question about a rattling tower of machinery, and Splid was leaning over to reply, his attention momentarily away from Gussie. Pegleg leaned over and said, 'Run for it, boy!'

Gussie stood irresolute for a moment. He wanted to ask Pegleg why, if he was a spy, he was helping him get away. *Or was he helping him?* Perhaps it was all a trap. But there was such a look of desperate honesty in Pegleg's boiled eyes that it was impossible to disbelieve him.

'I don't want to defect!' said Pegleg. 'Remember, follow the pipes. Now *run!*' He put his hand out. There was something in it, but Gussie did not hang around to see what it was. He began to run. Pegleg grabbed Snell instead and shoved the something into his pocket.

Gussie had discovered that there was nowhere to run to. He merely stepped aside behind a machine. There was a narrow gap between it and the ship's side, and he began to work his way down it. His knees did not seem to want to support him, and his heart was knocking unpleasantly at his ribs. Until now, it had all seemed a little unreal. But suddenly, for the first time, he had focussed his mind round the idea that they were going to try to kill him.

Gussie came to a ladder. He started to climb. He looked round and saw a fat seaman trying to force his way down the narrow passage. He was stuck, his belly caught on the machinery. The sound of it roared in his ears as he came to a catwalk. As he started across the wall of the metal cavern, the roar of machinery softened and ran down in a dying whine into a silence so loud it hurt his ears. Then the shouting began. From

128

across the floor of the factory hold, men in black rubber caps and aprons converged on Gussie's catwalk. Splid was shouting directions. Gussie looked up. There was a man above him. He looked down. The stuck man had dislodged himself, and a thinner man was edging towards his ladder. He looked to the sides. A man was waiting at either end of the catwalk.

Now Gussie's mouth was dry. I'll wake up soon, he thought; but of course there would be no waking this time.

Splid yelled an instruction. Gussie ran at the man who was coming at him from astern, because he looked the smallest. He hit him with his shoulder to knock him out of the way, but he might as well have charged a brick wall. The man grunted and picked Gussie up, holding him above his head. Gussie could smell the fish on his apron. Fifteen feet below was the production line, with a trough full of fish guts sunk into the floor behind it – the trough that fed the fishmealer. Gussie wriggled frantically. Splid called out an order. The cavern spun. Gussie caught a glimpse of daylight from the half-open ramp door. Then he was falling.

He landed with a splash in three feet of fish guts, and struggled to his feet. The stink was revolting. There was a commotion and a shrill whimpering, and Snell cartwheeled over the horizon and plummeted into the trough. Gussie got his head above floor level. Splid was turning towards the huge machine. He raised his thumb and punched a red button. Under Gussie's feet, the floor of the trough gave a great lurch. He fell into the muck, unbalanced, and could not find his footing because the floor kept on moving. He tried to swim, but it was like swimming in thick porridge. Snell was screaming now and Gussie could see why. The trough led down to a door in the side of the machine. Inside the door, big knives of gleaming steel revolved on wheels, chopping at the contents of the trough.

The knives were coming closer. Gussie began to struggle, shouting against the noise of the machine . . .

The noise stopped. So did the floor of the trough. Gussie scrambled to his feet, scraping mackerel guts from his eyes.

Pegleg and Splid were standing by the ON button. They looked as if they were ballroom dancing, except that Pegleg's face was purple under the lights and Splid's legs were working like pistons as he tried to push Pegleg into the trough. Pegleg had hold of a stanchion, his fingers white. Gussie watched the knuckles gradually straighten. Then Splid grunted something to a sailor, and the sailor pushed the ON button and the belt started again. As Gussie went down into the muck he saw Splid smash at Pegleg's knuckles with his boot and they lurched and both fell into the trough right in front of the door with the knives. Then there was one terrible scream cut off sharply, and a dreadful grating and juddering and a smell of burning insulation, and the machine stopped.

Gussie raised his head. The men in black aprons were gathered round the door of the fish-mealer. They were silent. None of them was smiling. Snell floundered further along the trough. Gussie grabbed his wrist and pointed. Very softly, they walked towards the ramp door, dripping offal. Gussie knew what had happened and did not want to look, but look he did, as they went past. There was no sign of Splid. Pegleg was sitting up to his neck in the trough. His face was white and frightened. He tried to struggle up; nobody helped him, and he sat back, hard. Gussie saw that his tin leg was caught up in the terrible knives. His trousers were torn, and there were bright gouges in the metal. His eye caught Gussie's, and he jerked his head at the exit doors.

All this Gussie saw in less than a second, as the Fishco workers sat transfixed by the sight of the fishmealer and its occupant. He had no time to think. Instead, he started to run. Grabbing Snell by the arm, he wrenched him through the gap in the doors and on to the stern ramp just as the shouting started again inside.

It was a small ramp, about the size of three or four snooker tables. Up it were hauled the bulging net bags of fish from the purse-seiners, the smaller ships that pulled the mackerel shoals from the sea. It was a slippery slope of riveted steel, and the wind howled over it like a chainsaw. Snell's eyes had a round, shocked look. Gussie clamped his fingers round a ring set in the steel and made him lie down, and shot a bolt across the double doors of the ramp.

'But there's nothing here,' Snell whimpered. 'Nothing.' He pressed his face into the wet plating. Hammers began crashing at the double doors. High on the rusty iron cliff above the ramp, there were hatchways and railings and the rungs of steps. Soon they would be thronged with men. Gussie looked around frantically. *Where was the dinghy*? There was plenty of blue sea, and blue sky now and long ragged feathers of

131

black and white cloud; but there was no dinghy.

Then he saw the thin terylene rope that hung straight down into the sea from the bottom rung of a ladder heading high into the air. The dinghy must have broken loose. His heart turned to lead, and his feet began to skid away towards the boiling wake. He grabbed at a rung of the ladder to steady himself, and gave the rope a despairing tug. Then he frowned. There was a weight at its bottom end. 'Come here,' he shouted at Snell. 'Come and help.' But Snell stayed face-down on his chosen strip of deck, awaiting whatever might befall. So Gussie had to loop his elbow through the rungs and haul in inch by painful inch on the rope. And after half a minute, what was on the end came into view. It looked like a black and white plastic barrel in a heavy clear polythene bag. Gussie started to grin until his face nearly split. 'Snell,' he roared. 'Get over here!'

Something in his voice made Snell look up. Two seamen were coming down the ladders now, slowly, purposefully. After all, there was nowhere to go from the stern ramp, except into the sea. Gussie stripped off the polythene and heaved out the barrel. He let it roll to the limit of its rope. As it touched the water, it split in half. From the halves there blossomed a huge yellow flower that hissed and swelled until it skated over the ship's wake. The men on the ladders shouted and sped up.

'Come *ON*!' yelled Gussie to Snell.

## 13

The radio is a very wonderful thing. Maurice's message had passed rapidly to the coastguard, who had refused to believe a word of it. But a man in the coastguard sometimes played chess with Maurice, so he had told a chap from RAF St Mawgan to watch out for funny stuff with foreign factory ships, and since the chap was an Intelligence Officer he in his turn had dropped a word to the pilot of one of the Nimrod early-warning-and-rescue 'planes on the morning patrol. And the pilot had taken a little time out to shadow the factory ship just before it left British territorial waters, which was how it came to be that the co-pilot, looking out of the starboard cockpit window as the plane banked at ten thousand feet above the rusty hulk of the factory ship, said 'Cor, stone me!' as the life-raft swelled in her wake. From up here it looked like a tiny yellow O, but Nimrod crews do a lot of air-sea rescue and can spot a life raft on a night as dark as a blacked-out coal cellar. The pilot said, 'Going down,' and the Nimrod stood on one wing, side-slipped away, and dived. On the first pass her belly missed the after-deck of the factory ship by twenty-five feet, and one of the men on the ladders dropped the gun with which he was about to let air out of the dinghy. By the second pass, Gussie had the tow-line unfastened, and the dinghy was bobbing free, and the Nimrod was radioing the air-sea rescue choppers on the emergency frequency.

The factory ship was a shrinking rust-brown blob on the horizon. The life-raft swooped and slid on the flanks of the huge navy-blue waves. On their crests, the wind still roared. In the troughs, it was as calm and quiet as a hidden valley. After five minutes, distant rotors clattered. Snell said, in the silence of a trough: 'About what happened on the ship. I mean when you escaped and I told you to come back. Of course I was making a plan of my own . . .' The words were torn away by the wind.

'Of course you were,' said Gussie, in the next trough. He fixed his eyes on Snell's spectacles, behind which the pebbly orbs shifted uneasily. 'And in the excitement of hearing that Grannie and I are staying on Tresco and not going to no

Bide-a-Wee Homes or Uncle Guys, I have clean forgotten everything except how brave you were.'

Snell made a face as if he had just sucked a lemon. But in the end he nodded.

The rotors came closer. As Gussie watched the yellow Sea King with RESCUE painted on its flank, he thought of Pegleg. It was difficult to remember Pegleg the spy, somehow. Easier to remember Pegleg who had saved his life, and to feel sad at the thought of him being carried off to wherever his sinister contacts in Fishco were taking him.

The chopper was overhead now, lashing the water with the downdraught from its rotors. The noise was appalling.

'Poor Pegleg,' said Gussie to himself.

'Blood transfusion,' groaned Welfare Snell as they carried him in at the Emergency entrance. 'Saline drips. I'm dying.' He twisted on the stretcher. Something dug into his hip. He put his hand in his pocket and pulled out a cassette tape wrapped in polythene. 'Goodness me!' said Snell, sitting up rather rapidly for one in need of transfusion and drips.

'Stop joggling,' said the man at the back of the stretcher.

'Hah,' snorted Snell. The light of superiority had returned to his eye, and his spectacles positively gleamed. 'Drive this stretcher to MI5!'

'Barmy as a filing cabinet,' said the stretcher man.

'Or anyway the police,' said Snell, realizing he was not on TV.

'They'll be in to see you,' said the stretcher man. 'Never fear.'

When Gussie awoke, he was in a white bed with sun streaming over slate roofs and granite walls outside. The sky was blue, and a couple of firecrests were bouncing over a *pittosporum* hedge. He shut his eyes again. There was a smell of coffee in the room, with a tinge of something slightly like petrol. Rum.

'Maurice?' he said.

Maurice was there, in a wheelchair. So was Grannie Dole. Later, Mr Hulbert dropped in. So did Dark, looking as furtive as he always did in the presence of grown-ups. At first, Gussie was glad to see them all. But then he found out why they had come.

They had come to say goodbye.

It seemed (Maurice explained) that Welfare Snell had done more than simply guard Gussie from murderous spymasters with his own life. In addition, he had wrested from a master spy a tape containing many secrets on their way into enemy hands. Snell was now a hero. Gussie was to be allowed to recover from his ordeal in the hospital. He was then to proceed immediately to Plymouth, where his Uncle Guy would be waiting.

Gussie told them what had happened. After that there was nothing to say. There was nobody else in the ward, so they had it to themselves, and they sat in companionable silence, knowing that it would be the last time they would be together for ages.

At eleven o'clock, the door opened and Snell came in. He was a gleaming Snell, wiped clean of offal, his spectacles polished to a high lustre and

136

his bony hands writhing over each other like wrestling tarantulas. 'Well, well, well, well,' said Snell. 'All together, I see.'

'You're not welcome here, nanny goat,' said Grannie Dole.

'Tut,' said Snell with ghastly jollity. 'Soon knock that out of you at the Bide-a-Wee, Gran!'

'Mrs Dole, to you,' said Grannie Dole. 'Watch your manners.'

Snell laughed lightly, as if to say that silly old women *would* be silly old women. 'Well, I expect you'd like to know the arrangements made for your reception at Plymouth,' he said to Gussie. 'Your Uncle Guy's got a new Executive Ford Granada. He'll take you to the shops; get you a couple of nice suits. Then he'll show you the school. He knows you'll be happy there. And a friend of his says that if you do well there'll be a space on the production line at his factory when you leave school. They make simulated-teak formica salad bowls, very . . . '

'Is this Mr Smith's room?' said a small man in the doorway.

Snell said, 'Kindly do not interrupt. I am here on Council business . . . '

'Oh,' said the small man, with withering coldness. 'You must be Snell. I'm, well, call me Robinson, MI5.'

Snell straightened his tie and smoothed his hair. 'About the tape,' he said.

'About the tape,' said the man. 'We've listened to it.'

Snell preened like a stag. 'It was nothing,' he said 'A little perseverance—'

'Shut up,' said the small man. 'I want to play it to you.'

'But it's just birdwatching notes,' said Gussie.

'Nope. The birdwatching notes were there. But there was an ultrasonic track as well.' The small man's eyes were kindly as he looked at Gussie. 'On the ultrasonic track were full details of . . . well, it doesn't matter what but we're very pleased that Mr Hopcraft didn't take it with him.' He frowned. 'Funny chap, Hopcraft.' Pulling a miniature cassette machine from his pocket, he pressed the ON button.

Pegleg's voice came out of the speakers.

'By the time you hear this I'll be well on my way,' it said. 'If you hear it all it means that Gussie Smith got away, which I must say delights me.' The taped voice sighed heavily. 'Thing is, I don't want to go. Realized as soon as I met Splid. Things have changed since my youth. And I don't like the idea of young Smith getting killed as a result of me. So I've arranged for him to escape, and because he's a decent young chap he'll probably insist on taking that reptile Snell with him. A word about Snell. He has conducted himself throughout with a cringing cowardice that makes rats look plucky. If he gets out of this with his skin, he'll have Gussie Smith to thank, and I bet he'll be ungrateful. It is people like Snell who have made people like Splid possible.'

Snell clutched at the end of the bed.

'I am recording this in my cabin, over the top of some of the information I was, um, exporting,' said Pegleg's voice. 'I have left the rest of it on. It has not been copied, though there's no reason you should believe that. I have tethered a life-raft to the ship's ramp. Soon, I shall go down to the factory hold with Splid. Then we shall see what we shall see.'

138

'That's it,' said the man from MI5. 'Well, Mr Snell?'

But Snell had gone.

'Pity,' said the man from MI5. 'I wanted to tell him about his new posting. He obviously needs to learn about islands, so I've arranged for him to be transferred to Freezer. It's near the Antarctic. Actually,' he said, 'it's not a real island. More like an iceberg, really. Well, I must be getting on. You'll find that your Uncle Guy's not expecting you any more. And I'm afraid your place at the Bide-a-Wee Home has been filled, Mrs Dole. So you'll just have to go back to Tresco. D'you mind? No? Didn't think you would.' He headed for the door and went out. Ten seconds later he poked his head round and said, 'By the way, sorry about your boat. Denis Jenkins is building you a new one, though. Go and have a look when you're up. Twenty foot, pine on oak, Lister diesel. All right?' He vanished.

Gussie squinted at the closed door. The sunlight seemed very bright, all of a sudden. It lit up the faces of Maurice and Dark and, best of all, Grannie Dole. She had got hold of a bottle of rum from somewhere and was waving it above her head, muttering blessings. It lit up a future with a new boat and without Welfare Snell.

'All *right*!' said Gussie to the closed door.


THE END

**TOM'S SAUSAGE LION**
by Michael Morpurgo

It was Christmas Eve when Tom first saw the lion. His mother had sent him out to fetch logs – and there was the lion padding through the orchard with a string of sausages in its mouth! Tom couldn't believe his eyes and, worst still, when he rushed indoors to tell them, his family didn't believe him either.

There *was* a lion. Tom knew there was, knew that he hadn't dreamed it. So he sat up, night after night, waiting for the lion to return . . .

0 552 524182

**CORGI BOOKS**

**LIVING FIRE AND OTHER S.F. STORIES**
by Nicholas Fisk

'All at once the Alien was there, standing beside
him! It had moved on silent feet, with incredible
stealth, seeking out human company. Zigger
made no move, showed no surprise. He was used
to alien beings. Some flew, some scuttled, some
crawled. Some even lived underground.'

But, like many of the stories in this new collection from Nicholas Fisk, Zigger's encounter
with the mysterious Alien is not quite what it
seems. Distant planets, weird creatures and
tales from beyond the stars are gathered here to
be much enjoyed by readers with questing
imaginations and a taste for adventure!

0 552 524530

**CORGI BOOKS**

**MANY HAPPY RETURNS AND
OTHER STORIES**
by Kathryn Cave

Alice loathes all her birthday presents on sight
and finds a hilarious way of dealing with
them . . .

Cousin Roderick comes to stay and causes chaos
until a spider provides an unusual solution . . .

The dreaded Mrs Bannerman terrorizes her
class when mystery messages from 'Billy
Molloy' appear on the blackboard. Who wrote
them?

And just what *are* James and Mary going to do
about the dinosaur in their garden?

These are just a few of the extremely funny and
perceptive stories in this new collection from
Kathryn Cave, author of the highly popular
*Dragonrise*.

0 552 524344

**CORGI BOOKS**

If you would like to receive a Newsletter about our new Children's books, just fill in the coupon below with your name and address (or copy it onto a separate piece of paper if you don't want to spoil your book) and send it to:

**The Children's Books Editor**
**Young Corgi Books**
**61–63 Uxbridge Road**
**Ealing**
**London W5 5SA**

Please send me a Children's Newsletter:

Name: ..................................................................................

Address: ..............................................................................

...............................................................................................

...............................................................................................

All Children's Books are available at your bookshop or newsagent, or can be ordered from the following address:
Corgi/Bantam Books,
Cash Sales Department,
P.O. Box 11, Falmouth, Cornwall TR10 9EN

Please send a cheque or postal order (no currency) and allow 60p for postage and packing for the first book plus 25p for the second book and 15p for each additional book ordered up to a maximum charge of £1.90 in UK.

B.F.P.O. customers please allow 60p for the first book, 25p for the second book plus 15p per copy for the next 7 books, thereafter 9p per book.

Overseas customers, including Eire, please allow £1.25 for postage and packing for the first book, 75p for the second book, and 28p for each subsequent title ordered.